SPONTANEOUS JUSTICE

SPONTANEOUS JUSTICE

THE UNBELIEVABLE MR. BROWNSTONE™ BOOK FIFTEEN

MICHAEL ANDERLE

DISRUPTIVE IMAGINATION®

LMBPN Publishing
PMB 196, 2540 South Maryland Pkwy
Las Vegas, NV 89109

First US edition, December 2019
Version 1.01, January 2021

SPONTANEOUS JUSTICE TEAM

Special Thanks
to Mike Ross
for BBQ Consulting
Jessie Rae's BBQ - Las Vegas, NV

Thanks to the JIT Readers

John Ashmore
Misty Roa
Diane L. Smith
Micky Cocker
Angel LaVey
Keith Verret
James Caplan
Jeff Eaton
Kelly O'Donnell
Daniel Weigert
Peter Manis
Paul Westman
Larry Omans

If I've missed anyone, please let me know!

Editor
Lynne Stiegler

To Family, Friends and
Those Who Love
to Read.
May We All Enjoy Grace
to Live the Life We Are
Called.

CHAPTER ONE

The dark-haired woman in front of James adjusted her cat-eye glasses and frowned at the computer in front of her.

"Mr. Brownstone, is it?" She glanced at him, a dubious look on her face as she took in the large tattooed man in front of her.

Why is she looking at me like that? James thought.

James' gaze dipped to the bronze nameplate on her desk: MARY WINTERS, TWP. He was in the right place, so why was the woman acting like she'd had too spicy a lunch and needed to run to the bathroom?

He nodded. "Yeah, that's me. James Brownstone. When I made the appointment, they told me just to put everything in the Notes section, and you'd read that over and let me know what was useful. If you need to know something else, I can tell you. I've never done this kind of thing before. Sorry if I screwed something up." He shrugged.

Mary smiled softly and folded her hands on her broad

oak desk. It was covered with pictures of various men and women at their weddings.

"Perhaps I'm misunderstanding the information you passed along to me, Mr. Brownstone, but from what I can tell, you haven't even asked your girlfriend to marry you yet."

"Yeah, still working on the perfect fu...perfect proposal."

She seems like the kind of woman who might get upset if I'm a little too much me, but I need her help, so I better tone it down. At least until she gives me the info I need.

"Technically," he continued, "I kind of did start to propose, but she wanted something more special than what I was doing, which was just asking, but maybe she was mad because I didn't have a ring yet? I get that not having a ring was a big screw-up, but you know, like I said, I'm inexperienced."

James had encountered few things in his life as complicated as understanding Shay's wants and desires. From the beginning, her reactions had confused him.

"I...see." Mary pursed her lips tightly, and something approaching panic appeared in her eyes.

What is her deal? Maybe she really does need to go to the bathroom.

"And that's a good thing," James continued. "She needs something special because she's special." He shrugged. "And I'm still trying to figure all that out. I've been listening to podcasts, but they aren't very useful. It's the same sh...advice over and over, but they don't give me specific examples. Not ones that apply to her and me, anyway, which is why I'm here right now."

The woman chuckled nervously. "I understand how frustrating that must be, Mr. Brownstone, and it sounds like you've had a confusing time of it." Her mouth made an O. "Wait, are you the James Brownstone who is the bounty hunter? From the amusement park incident? I don't pay much attention to crime. It's too depressing, but I did hear about that on the news."

"Yeah, that's me. Is that a problem?" James grunted. Not a good time for his reputation to interfere.

Mary shook her head. "No, I was just rather impressed with your work and fascinated to learn about the size of your bounties. I didn't realize before hearing about it on the news how much money some bounty hunters make." Her smile grew wider and hungrier.

Yeah, that's what greed looks like, all right. Is that what her attitude was about? She thought I was a drifter bum who couldn't afford her services? Whatever. I can pay.

James reached into his pocket to pull out the shield ring and set it on the table. "I scored a ring already. I learned from that mistake."

Mary leaned forward to examine the ring. She tilted her head. "Is this jade?"

James nodded. "Yeah. It's over a thousand years old."

"That's non-traditional for weddings in this part of the world." Mary sighed. "An antique is an impressive choice, but you might consider something more traditional."

"Oh, that's just the engagement ring. I forgot to mention that it's magic. She needed a new shield ring, and this one won't crap out on her like the others." James shrugged. "That's something you don't want to have to deal with in the middle of a fight. I mean, if you know you're

3

not gonna have decent armor or shields, you can adjust your tactics, but if you think you have and it turns bad, that's gonna get you hurt. Maybe killed."

Mary blinked. "Oh, I see. That's certainly a...concern, depending on one's lifestyle. Um, and is your prospective fiancée a woman who will find a non-traditional ring acceptable? I mean, men often think that non-traditional rings and plans will excite women, but they underestimate how important connecting with decades and centuries of tradition can be. Many women want a wedding like their mother's and grandmother's, just more extravagant."

James shrugged. The ring was the one thing he *didn't* doubt.

"Yeah, totally fine. She's kind of non-traditional about everything, which is why I'm having a problem. You know, all the podcasts I've listened to have these cutesy ideas, and none of them make any sense for her. She's not the kind of woman who likes frilly cutesy crap, and she hates her mom. They don't even talk anymore."

Mary turned to tap notes into her computer. "Unfortunate, but I *will* say that the fewer in-laws involved, the greater control the bride tends to have over her own wedding. That can definitely be a major advantage."

James frowned. "Traditional, huh? She does like expensive restaurants that don't have barbeque. That's pretty traditional."

Mary nodded. "I suppose you could say that." She cleared her throat. "I wouldn't recommend barbeque for your wedding meal. I was just concerned about your ring. You said that was the engagement ring. What about the wedding ring? Is it more traditional?"

James shook his head. "I still haven't gotten the wedding ring. The jade ring's just the engagement ring, but it has a matching pendant. You think that would work? Or do I have to have another ring?" He frowned. "I'm figuring I do according to what the podcasts told me. And Alison, Maria, Kathy, and Charlyce told me that too. Nana Garfield threatened to slap me upside my head when I said I was thinking about not getting a wedding ring."

Mary stared at James, disbelief on her face. "I agree with all those women. Mr. Brownstone. I assure you that even if the lucky woman is extremely non-traditional, you still should err on the side of caution in making sure you have both a wedding ring and an engagement ring." She offered James a tight smile. "But again, I'm confused. This is her engagement ring, which means you haven't even proposed, and what you've said seems to indicate that as well. Is that a correct summation of your current situation vis-à-vis your prospective bride?"

James grunted. "Kind of? Like I said, I tried to propose to her once, but it wasn't planned, and she stopped me. She didn't say no, she just said she wanted it to be...more special. So now I'm trying to figure out how to propose and make it special. I've tried talking to all the women I know, and everyone keeps feeding me lines about 'showing that I care and know what Shay would want.'"

"And this Shay is your intended fiancée, I take it?"

"Yeah, but it's been months now. I've listened to so many podcasts and watched a bunch of videos on the internet with different proposals." James groaned. "I even watched every episode of *The World's Best Proposals*, and I *still* don't have any idea what might work. This whole thing is getting fucking epically complicated."

Mary gasped, and her face reddened.

"Uh, sorry." James grunted and shrugged. "When I tried to propose to her, she told me the proposal needed to be fucking epic. That was what I meant by special before, but I'm not good at this kind of thing. It's been hard for me to figure out, even with help, so that's why I've come to you. You're an expert, so I figured you could help me."

"I see. This Shay certainly seems like a…very colorful woman. I can see how you two will get on well together."

James chuckled. "You could say that. She's the perfect woman for me."

Mary stared at James for a few seconds. "That much I can tell without having even met her." She sighed and shook her head. "Now, at this agency, we pride ourselves on creating the best and most involved—epic, if you will—wedding experiences for all our clients. You'll find our satisfaction ratings and reviews are some of the best in LA for wedding planners, and while I'm sure we could satisfy your lovely Shay's wedding requirements, no matter how non-traditional or epic, there's a fundamental problem that needs to be addressed first."

"What? Don't worry about the wedding ring thing. I'm gonna make that easy on myself. Once I propose, I'll make her pick one out." James shrugged. "I did the thoughtful thing with the engagement ring, and Shay might be pushing me on this proposal, but she's not gonna torture me when it comes to the wedding." He winced. "I hope. I think she'll get how much I've tried. Taking down the

Drow queen was easier than figuring out this proposal has been so far."

Mary waved her hands in front of her, an exasperated expression taking over her face. "No, no. I mean yes, that's, well, that *is* an issue, but it's not the issue I'm talking about." She pinched the bridge of her nose and took a few deep breaths. "Mr. Brownstone, I'm a wedding planner, not a proposal planner. Given the nature of the proposal experience, my particular skill set isn't suited to helping a couple in that kind of situation, and you'll find that's the case with most people in my profession. Typically, by the time you're coming to someone like me, you've already proposed, and both members of the couple are talking with me. I simply am not the person you need to help you with your particular problem."

James frowned. "You can't help me with the proposal?"

"Not in the way you probably want, and not much more than your various other female friends probably have." Mary managed a tight smile. "I *will* note that the advice you have received is good. You need to tailor your proposal to Shay's personality and desires. Don't worry. After she says yes, all your stress will go away. *I* will make all your stress go away." Another too-hungry smile appeared on her face. "At that point, I'll take care of everything else. I'll help guide the entire wedding-planning process so it's an enjoyable experience and not a cause for concern. You won't have to watch shows or listen to podcasts. This agency is a one-stop shop for wedding planning."

James grabbed the ring from the desk and slipped it back into his pocket. "Damn. Wasted your time and mine." He stood and headed toward the door. "Sorry about that."

"Mr. Brownstone," Mary called.

James looked over his shoulder. "Yeah?"

Her too-sweet smile almost made him shudder.

"I'm sure you'll figure it out," Mary replied, "and once you do, I would encourage you to make another appointment for my services. As you're already experiencing, these things can be taxing. It's best to leave it to an expert. As good as you are at bounty hunting, that's how good I am at wedding planning. Please note that our agency has agreements with several Oriceran contractors. We can literally make your wedding magical."

James opened the door and stepped through. "I'll keep that in mind." He shut it behind him. "Just need to find a fucking proposal expert first."

Fifteen minutes on the road in his rumbling F-350 helped shake some of the tension out of James' shoulders. Even if he'd failed to get useful professional advice about his proposal, it wasn't as if Shay was riding him about it, or at least not yet.

But how long is she gonna wait? Six months? A year? Two years? How long will it take before I get this shit figured out? Fuck, it would have been easier if she just told me what she wanted me to do. I don't know anything about romance. She knows that.

James let out a low growl. Kicking down a door and punching a man through a window was simple and straightforward, and sometimes even fun, depending on the day. Figuring out what a woman wanted was torturous and complicated almost all the time.

"Okay," he mumbled to himself. "I've talked to almost every woman I know well, and everyone's given me the same advice, but I still need a specialist who knows about this stuff and won't get tripped up over Shay wanting non-traditional shit, whatever the fuck that means."

James switched lanes after a quick mirror check, frowning for a second at a driver who looked suspiciously like King Pyro.

Have I pounded so many people into the pavement that I can't help but see the bastards everywhere I go now?

After taking a turn a little hard and leaving the Pyro doppelganger behind, James smiled at a sudden flash of inspiration. If conventional, traditional help was failing him, maybe it was time to bring in non-conventional and non-traditional help—someone who was all about romantic ideas and inspiring men.

James turned into a liquor store parking lot and looked through the window to make sure no assholes were robbing the place before pulling out his phone. He searched through the contacts until he found the number for Anna Forsythe and dialed.

"We're sorry," came a soft female voice. "The number you have dialed is out of service. Please hang up, check the number, and dial again."

James grunted and hit the End button, then called Tyler immediately. This was a good idea, and he wasn't going to let a bad phone number kill it.

"What's up, Brownstone?" Tyler answered. "I'm kind of

in the middle of something, so if this doesn't involve making money, can it wait?"

Fucker never changes, does he?

"It involves me not being pissed off," James rumbled, "and that means less chance of you needing to fix something. Doors cost money to replace."

Tyler snorted. "Fine. What is it?"

"Anna Forsythe. I need to get a hold of her, but her number doesn't work anymore." James looked up as a news helicopter flew overhead. Always something happening in LA.

"Yeah, she's got personal reasons for that, from what I hear." Tyler sighed. "I'll give you her number if you guarantee me this isn't about you going after her. I don't care what bullshit some angry ex-wife fed you, she doesn't deserve that. She's a nice woman who makes it clear what she offers in exchange for shit given freely."

James grunted. "Nothing like that. I just need her help with something. Not that Bard of Filth crap."

Tyler snickered. "Let me guess, is this about your proposal? It's sad, Brownstone. By the time this whole thing is over, you'll have asked half the people in LA for advice. Maybe you should go on the internet and crowd-source the advice. Huh. You know, if you were willing to do that, I've got a few ideas about how we could monetize that. We can give it a cool name. Sell advertising during the whole thing."

"Fuck off, Tyler. Not auctioning my proposal or whatever." James grunted. "And, yeah, Anna knows her shit about romance, given what she is, I figure, so maybe she can help. Do you know how to get hold of her or not?"

"Yeah, yeah, I know her number. Consider this an early wedding present, and don't say I've never done anything for you." Tyler rattled off the number.

James' memory made it unnecessary to write it down or enter it into his phone. His contact list was for dialing ease, not necessity.

"Thanks," James replied.

"Sure thing, Brownstone," Tyler replied. "Just remember when the big day comes who helped you, especially if that sexy little woman's advice works."

"I'll keep that shit in mind next time I get an urge to kick in your door." James ended the call.

He sat in the parking lot for a minute staring down at his phone.

Do I really want to ask her? I owe her for her help last time, and who knows how she might want to collect? She seemed okay, but just being around her messed with my head. And even if I bonded with Whispy, he doesn't seem to help as much against stuff that messes with my head.

James sighed. He was running out of options, as well as useful romance advice podcasts that didn't annoy the ever-living shit out of him with weak-ass advice that didn't apply to him and Shay. He dialed Anna.

One ring. Two rings. Three rings. Four rings. It wouldn't be long before it went to voicemail.

Maybe this is for the best.

"An unexpected but perhaps fortuitous call, Mr. Brownstone," Anna answered in a sultry voice.

James frowned. "What do you mean by that?"

"Let's just say it's been far too long, and I found you interesting during our last encounter. Perhaps you could come and visit, hmm? It'd be nice to see you again, if only to appreciate the glory of your form and your amusing demeanor."

Maybe this shit was a mistake.

James frowned. "This isn't some succubus seduction shit, is it?"

"I'm not a succubus. I'm a leanan sidhe. I can assure you I don't serve your precious Satan, Mr. Brownstone. From what I can tell from *Paradise Lost,* he's quite the bore." Anna let out a soft laugh. "If you recall, I explained before that you're not really my type. Besides, you're the one who called me, so obviously you have an interest in speaking to me."

James took a deep breath through his nose and slowly let it out through his mouth. "You're right. Sorry. I needed your advice on something. Romance shit."

"I see. All the more reason to visit in person, since I incidentally wanted to collect on the little favor you already owe me, and it sounds as if you're going to acquire more debt. After all, my advice does have value."

"How did you want to collect on my debt, exactly?" James furrowed his brow, his stomach tightening.

The Celtic faerie had claimed he wasn't her type, and that made sense given her interest in artistic men, but he also didn't want to have to explain to Shay why some leanan sidhe might call him up in the middle of the night and flirt with him.

"Whatever it is you're thinking, Mr. Brownstone, I assure you that you're wrong," Anna replied, her voice thick with amusement as if she could read his thoughts. "Trust me, the task I have in mind is particularly well suited for your normal everyday talents, which I admit are almost at the level of art."

"What the fuck does that mean?"

Anna sighed. "I prefer to discuss this matter in person, but I can assure you, you'll find it an easy way to discharge your past and soon-to-be-incurred debt, and it won't bother you in the slightest nor trouble your conscience, judging by your current lifestyle."

A normal woman was difficult enough to understand, but this woman was enjoying messing with him far too much.

James frowned at his phone.

Damn it. She's right. I called her, and I've dealt with her before, so I know what to expect. If she wants sex, there are thousands of other guys she could call.

"Okay," James replied with a growling rumble. "I'll stop by your place tomorrow. We'll chat there."

"I've got a better idea," Anna replied. "Take me out to lunch. There's an Italian place I've been meaning to try. I'll text you the time and place later. I'll meet you there, so you don't have to feel like you're walking into the spider's web."

James grunted. "Fine."

"Until then." Anna ended the call with a final chuckle.

What the fuck did I just get myself into?

CHAPTER TWO

S hay settled into a chair and smiled at her department head, who was sitting behind his desk. The man gave her a nervous smile back, his hands folded and his face a little too red. She doubted that he'd pounded shots at lunch.

She laughed. "Damn, Alan, relax. You look like you just heard they're going to close the whole department and make you go teach at traffic school."

Alan took a deep breath and adjusted his bowtie. "I heard a rumor, a very disturbing rumor, and it's been worrying me. Vexing me, if you will."

"Vexing?" Seriously?

"Rumor?" Shay frowned. "About what, exactly?"

Shit. There's no way this guy can connect me with tomb raiding. He doesn't even do field work anymore, let alone stay in touch with the dark side of archaeology and artifact collection. It's not like the people who know I'm Aletheia would call up a stuffed shirt like Alan to chat about it.

Shay's frown deepened. Unless Erin North had delivered a counter-attack to disrupt Shay's life before faking her own death?

Alan lifted his chin as if trying to summon his courage. "The rumor is that you are planning on leaving for the University of Wyoming. That they offered you a full professorship and a fast track to tenure."

"Huh?" Shay chuckled and shook her head. "I don't think I'd do well in Wyoming. Gets too cold in the winter, and I'm really more of a big city kind of woman."

Alan let out a long sigh of relief. "That's what I was thinking as well, but there's been a lot of chatter about it, so I just wanted to be sure. When you said you wanted to have a meeting with me, I assumed it was to talk about you leaving."

Shay smirked. "There's been a lot of chatter about me moving to Wyoming?"

He replied with a curt nod as if everyone in the department sat around having discussions about Shay and her interest in random states all day long.

Who knows, maybe they do. It's tough being as badass and impressive in all parts of life as I am.

Shay cleared her throat. "Okay, here's a situation where a kernel of truth has been twisted beyond recognition, but there's still a kernel of truth."

Alan's eyes widened. "Kernel of truth?" he squeaked.

Shay resisted a laugh. The man spent most of the last year acting smug toward her, and now he looked like he was going to wet his pants because he thought she might be moving to Wyoming.

Finally learning not to take things for granted, huh?

Alan slumped in his chair and scrubbed a hand over his

face. "If you're not going to Wyoming, then where… No, no, no. Not USC. Anywhere but USC. I'll never hear the end of it from them at the next conference. They've already poached two people from my department in the last five years."

Shay rolled her eyes. "You're that worried about losing me? To be honest, I didn't think you cared that much about me."

Alan took a few more deep breaths and offered her a forced smile. "Your guest lectures are some of the most popular among students in both the archaeology and history departments. Did you know enrollment is up in both majors? Departmental surveys indicate a strong correlation with your lectures and people selecting the majors. One incoming freshman for next year specifically mentioned you in their admissions essay." He leaned forward, some of his confidence returning to his face. "Suffice it to say, we understand the value of your lectures for generating student interest in majors that normally aren't considered as sexy as some of the other majors on campus."

"Really? People don't care that half of what we know about human civilization is a lie, and we're still coming to grips with that in ways that might take decades more, if not centuries, to fully appreciate? That's not enough to get them interested in archaeology and history unless I give a fancy speech about it?" Shay snorted. Why were so many people so myopic?

Alan shrugged. "I don't disagree with you, Shay. I'm just telling you that it's been a hard sell, and we've been worried about budget cuts. Because of some of the state funding shortfalls the last few years, all the state universities have been tightening up, and that's trickled down to us at the departmental level. We've had to be creative with graduate funding, given the pinch on federal grants for students in our fields." He smiled. "But you're helping change that for our department and our sister department. More students being interested gives us ammo to help fight off the people trying to take our funding. In this battle, they'll have to go sniffing for weaker prey." He smirked, obviously pleased with his metaphor.

Shay grinned. When she'd asked for the meeting with her department head, she'd thought what she was about to ask would be a harder fight, but he was giving her every weapon and argument she needed to win with ease.

Talk about your weak prey. You need to fight a little harder, Alan.

"So, it sounds to me like if I left this campus for whatever reason, you would be hurt in a big way?"

"I...I suppose you could say that." Alan's face paled and he swallowed, seemingly realizing his mistake.

Shay learned forward. "Then maybe we should talk about me doing something more than just giving guest lectures, like a permanent appointment and teaching a regular class or two."

Alan sighed. "Yes, but you see, the issue is...well, like I just said, it's budgetary. We've barely fought off the vultures, and justifying another full-time position is very, very difficult in this funding climate, especially since you're not bringing in any external funding. If you had a few grants, the situation would be very different, but as far as I've heard, you haven't even applied for any."

Shay resisted laughing in his face. In truth, her entire

official academic background was nothing but a complicated series of frauds and faked information, courtesy of
Peyton.

Funding? It wasn't as if she needed the money. Her
tomb raider career had been very lucrative, not even taking
into consideration her years as a professional killer, but
only being around for a few guest lectures meant she could
never achieve any sort of true permanency at the university. People valued others when they had to pay, so she was
going to make him cough up.

*I was supposed to retire to some tropical island somewhere,
but that was before I met James and Alison. That alien bitch
might have tricked me when it came to the lance, but her forty
million dollars was real enough. The joke's on her since the
weapon's pretty much useless now.*

Shay scratched her ear. "So let me get this straight…
you're desperately afraid I'm going to leave for another
university offering me a full-time position, but you're not
willing to provide me any sort of stability here? I'm going
to politely note this is at least a mixed message, if not
downright insulting."

Alan swallowed. "When you first came here, you said
you weren't interested in that sort of thing. We had an
understanding. You made it very clear, in fact."

"Come on, we're archaeologists. If there's one thing we
should both understand, it's that things and people
change." Shay frowned. "I've changed and my life's
changed, and I want a full-time position."

"That might seem advisable at first, but have you
thought through all the implications?" Alan adjusted his
bowtie again, beads of sweat forming on his forehead.

"Right now you get to concentrate on the fun aspects of being a professor. No grading, no managing graduate students, and you have much more time for your field research. If you start teaching, you're going to be tethered here, and from what I remember of your background, your teaching experience is limited."

Shay snorted. "I've proven that I can connect with students. You just got done telling me someone mentioned me in an admissions essay."

It took extreme self-control not to curse at him or laugh in his face.

"Yes, yes. I do not doubt that you can connect with students." Alan's gaze darted around nervously. "You don't get it, because you don't have to deal with students for lengthy periods in unpleasant situations. You only have to deal with them when you're teaching your fun guest lectures. Shay, they're *monsters*. Whiny, entitled little monsters."

Shay finally lost her fight and burst out laughing. "Monsters? No, a monster is a crystal squid or a giant spider, not some mouthy eighteen-year-old student."

Not that I can admit I've fought both those creatures.

"My point is," Alan replied, "that you're an archaeologist used to a slow pace in the field. Used to spending your time really getting to know a site and expanding your knowledge base." He shook his head. "Dealing with threatening and entitled students won't be the same. You might not be able to handle it. A semester as a teaching assistant during graduate school isn't the same thing as managing an entire class."

Unless I get a bunch of homicidal ice witches in my classes, I doubt I can't handle them. Wonder what Alan would say if I told him that?

Shay shrugged. "Could always see what USC has to say after all." She stood and grinned. "This isn't one of those 'Why buy the cow when you can get the milk for free?' situations, Alan. If you don't value me enough to give me a permanent position, I'll move on. I have to do what's best for my career." She spun on her heel and headed for the door.

"Shay, wait!"

She stopped and looked over her shoulder at him. "What?"

"I'll see what I can do." Alan hung his head, his face pale. "But at the earliest, it wouldn't be until fall semester. Can we still count on you for summer lectures?"

"As long as you're working on things, I can be patient." Shay continued toward the door. "Just ask my boyfriend."

The front door opened and Shay looked up. James stepped through, leashed dog trailing behind. Thomas wandered in after the bounty hunter, his tail wagging furiously as it always did after his post-dinner walk with James. His master knelt and removed the leash.

The dog barked and rushed into the living room where he greeted Shay, then circled three times beside James' recliner before lying down. James hung the leash up on the coat rack by the door.

They both always look so happy when they come home, Shay thought.

James smiled at Shay, who was on the couch looking at her phone. "Hey, Shay! You just get home?"

"Nope. About forty-five minutes ago." Shay set her phone down, finishing for the moment her idle perusal of the USC archaeology department's webpage. "Even if you left right before I got here, you took a damned long time. Did Mrs. Garth ambush you again to talk about how her grandson isn't married yet? The way she talks, the guy is the hottest smart rich man to ever live, and he should be the next king of Oriceran. I think sometimes she's trying to convince me to leave you for him."

"I doubt most men could handle you. Probably not even the king of Oriceran."

Shay smirked. "You're right about that."

James nodded toward Thomas. "He just needed a while to go. Maybe he needs more fiber and shit."

"More fiber would help him shit, sure." Shay glanced back down at her phone for a moment, then back up at James. "Just so you know, I talked to my department head today about teaching a regular class and getting a permanent position. Made it clear that I don't want to be only a guest lecturer, and that if he doesn't play ball, I'll consider going to another place."

James moved over to his recliner and dropped into it. He extended the footrest. "Yeah? You've been thinking about that for a while."

Shay shook her head. "But this isn't just theorizing about it. I basically forced him into a corner and demanded a permanent job after he tried to feed me a bunch of bullshit about the budget." She grinned. "Oh, it was fun. I remember when he thought he could push me around. I always wanted to punch him in his fucking smug face, but now I have the weapon of popularity. Who knew? Not quite as satisfying as punching a man in the face or throat, but it's nice in its own way. What do you think?"

James rubbed his chin. "I'm not sure if punching a guy in the face is more satisfying than kicking or shooting them. Depends on the guy."

"I meant about the job." Shay laughed.

"Oh, I think it's a good idea." James stretched, his thick muscles straining against his shirt.

Shay almost licked her lips at the sight. It was nice having the Prince of Pec-town as a boyfriend. "Really?"

"Yeah, not like we're moving anywhere, and you get restless. Sounds like a good way to work off restless energy without having to kill someone, but are you sure about this? Wouldn't it make it harder to go on raids? I mean, it's not like you do them just for money, right? Satisfaction and shit, like me and barbeque."

"I've been thinking a lot about that, and you're right, I don't do them just for money, but I also don't have to do so many. I have piles of money, and, yeah, it's expensive to maintain the warehouses and keep myself swimming in gear, but now I've got so many investments, I could probably never do a tomb raid again and live a swanky lifestyle until I die from natural causes." Shay laughed. "Dying from natural causes? Now there's something I never thought would happen. The point is, maybe it's time to finally let civilization win. At least for a little while."

She looked at the stone-faced James. Maybe *he* needed more fiber. Or at least he needed to laugh at her jokes more.

"Let civilization win?" he echoed.

Shay nodded. "I faked my death because of the cartel, and we destroyed the cartel. Durand's dead. Snegurka's dead, and we've stopped poking the government about their alien projects. If we can track down Erin and take her down, there will be no major threats on my end. I can have a semi-normal life where I'm not always looking over my shoulder." She furrowed her brow. "As much as an ex-professional-killer turned-tomb-raider who lives with her alien boyfriend can have a normal life."

James grunted. "Sounds good, except for that shit with the alien bitch. Heather hasn't found anything since the plane crash."

"Neither has Peyton."

James shrugged. "Maybe she really *is* dead."

Shay snorted. "I'd love to believe that, but we don't have that kind of luck. This is one of those times where you're not going to get the simple life, even if she has been damned quiet these last few months. She's the only true threat to your peace, quiet, and barbeque, and to me."

"I agree, but it's not like we can do anything. If Heather and Peyton can't find anything, not like you or I are gonna be able to find shit."

Shay frowned. "What about Smite-Williams?"

"The Professor is asking around as quietly as he can since I explained everything to him, and he hasn't found anything, either." James grunted. "You know what, though? I don't know if I give a shit."

Shay raised an eyebrow. "You don't give a shit about an advanced alien hunting you who likely faked her own death just to throw us off her trail?"

James reached over to scratch behind Thomas' ears. "She's zero for two against me, and she's the one who faked her death to hide, not me. If she thought she had a chance, she would have come at me already. I think we just let Peyton and Heather do their thing. Eventually, she'll make a mistake, then we'll figure out where she is and handle her. Until then, we keep on carrying on."

"This is a mighty big threat to just ignore."

"Not ignoring it." James chuckled. "Just focusing on the shit that matters. Fuck that alien, and fuck any aliens who want to screw with us. I'm not gonna be afraid because they want to kill me. They'll have to get in line."

CHAPTER THREE

Johnny Lee leaned forward to scrutinize the mahjong tiles in front of him. His hand was utter crap, and he risked losing a lot of money. His luck was garbage that night, and he knew at least some of his men were letting him win so as not to piss him off, which made him angrier.

Fuck. Why do I even play this game? It always ends up pissing me off.

He frowned down at his plate of half-eaten dim sum. He had a crap hand and a bunch of food with the gentle flavor of a piece of paper, even after hiring a new chef. Considering how much he was paying, he should have been able to find a half-decent chef, even if most people were afraid to work for him as the local leader of the 25K Triad.

Johnny looked around at the men lounging at the tables and booths of Kowloon, his restaurant and primary base of operations. Both aspects were in need of improvement, even if he'd managed to expand the triad's presence in LA in recent months after a few unfortunate initial reversals.

I might gamble for shit and this food is terrible, but at least the business is coming along. That shit's going to get me recognized. I'll move up. Maybe I can even go back to San Francisco.

Murmurs and shouts swept through the restaurant, and Johnny lifted his head to see what the commotion was about.

What the fuck now?

He frowned.

One of his men stumbled through the door, blood and cuts all over his face. His blue suit jacket was shredded with long, narrow cuts. He collapsed to his knees once he cleared the door. The man was one of Johnny's main enforcers, Andy Chen.

Several men jumped up from nearby tables to run to him. Johnny stood and pushed his chair in. He maneuvered through the tables toward the wounded man, his brow furrowed in surprise and concern.

Fuck. Is she back?

Johnny frowned and cut through the air with his hand. "If you're not 25K, get the hell out of here now. If you haven't paid, don't worry—whatever you had is on me. All employees come back tomorrow morning. If I don't want you here, I'll put up signs, and you'll still be paid for your shifts."

A proper ruler had to take care of his people in good times and bad.

Half the people in the restaurant rose, exchanging nervous looks. They shuffled out, their attention locked on the wounded man. A few employees ran into the back to shout in Cantonese and Spanish. The kitchen employees streamed out after that.

Johnny grimaced as his bartender disappeared with the rest of the fleeing people. He really needed to train one of his men to do that job for situations like this. It was hard to know when you might need a nice mixed drink to cut the edge.

The wounded man pushed the other people off him, murmuring something under his breath.

Johnny closed and knelt in front of him. "Andy, what the fuck happened?"

Andy continued murmuring almost inaudibly.

Johnny leaned in to listen.

Andy stared down at his blood-covered hands. "She's coming. She's coming. She's coming."

The triad leader frowned and shook his man by the shoulders. "Who's coming? What the fuck happened? Where are the rest of the guys?" He looked around to confirm that only his men were left in the restaurant. They didn't need witnesses to 25K business.

She's *coming?*

Johnny's stomach knotted. There was one woman who'd messed with the triad when they'd first started pushing hard into LA. They'd had trouble with the dark-haired bitch a while back, but he'd thought they'd come to an understanding with her, and he hadn't run into her or her little gray-haired friend in a long time.

It didn't make any sense for the dark-haired bitch to come back. The last time they'd dealt with her, she'd traded with them for information.

Shit. Did someone mess with her little pet elf chick? If I shoot one of the guys responsible and apologize, maybe she'll leave the rest of us alone.

Johnny shook Andy again. "Who's coming? Is it the dark-haired bitch?"

Andy laughed manically. "No, she's a normal woman. We'd at least have a chance if it was the other one."

"Who the fuck are you talking about?" Johnny shouted. "And what happened to the other guys with you?"

Andy blinked several times. "They're all dead. She killed them. Cut them up like they were nothing. It's her. She's real—the Silver Ghost."

Concerned murmurs rippled around the room. Every man now stood in a rough semi-circle around Johnny and Andy.

No, this shit isn't happening.

Johnny swallowed. Andy was right. The triad leader would have preferred the dark-haired bitch to be the one hunting them rather than the Silver Ghost.

He took a few deep breaths, trying to focus. The worst thing he could do at that moment was show fear. It was time to be a leader, even if he didn't believe what he was about to say. Doubt was poison to men who had to risk their lives.

"The Silver Ghost's not real." Johnny stood to sweep the room with his harsh glare. "She's just an urban legend. Bullshit the cops probably made up last month, or even some other gangs trying to scare people out of LA. I'm not running from some fake legend of a vigilante." He reached inside his jacket and pulled out his gun. "We have no business calling ourselves 25K if we run from fucking words."

Andy laughed. "She's going to kill us all. She's going to chop our heads off."

One of the other men pointed at Andy. "Someone fucked him up. You saying words did that shit, Johnny?"

He snorted. "Some assholes musta ambushed him. It's a trick. Probably mindfucked him with magic or an artifact. If this Silver Ghost was real and such a badass, why is she jumping guys in alleys when they aren't expecting her? Plus, she's supposed to be in LA and Vegas, the rumors say? What the fuck is up with that? What kind of monster vigilante commutes on the 15 back and forth?"

"Brownstone does," another man offered, his gaze averted.

Johnny groaned. "Too many damned ghosts in LA. Silver Ghost. Granite Ghost." He let off a stream of invectives in Cantonese. "Brownstone's real. He's on video. He goes to fucking barbeque competitions. Where's the damned Silver Ghost, huh? All those phones and drones and no one's got actual pictures of her?" He put his gun on a table, grabbed Andy, and pulled him up by his lapels. "Get your shit together, man. This is a trick."

"You don't understand, Johnny." Andy wiped tears away. "She's coming. She only didn't kill me because I was supposed to deliver a message."

Johnny released Andy and shoved him back. The wounded gangster fell on his ass.

"What fucking message?" Johnny snarled.

Andy stared at his leader. "She's coming here in an hour for all of us. She said to get whatever weapons you want because she needs to test something. We can try to run, but if we do, she'll track us down and kill us slowly. If we stand

and fight, at least she'll honor our bravery by killing us fast."

The room filled with shouted curses. Cacophony reigned.

"Everyone shut the fuck up!" Johnny shouted.

The men fell silent.

The triad leader held up his gun again. "Ever since we let that dark-haired bitch push us around, we've had no balls. I don't give a fuck that some wizard mindfucked Andy. We're the fucking 25K Triad, and we're not going to let anyone push us out of LA. We fought our way in, and we've expanded our operations despite everybody from street gangs to the Russian Mafia coming at us." He snorted. "This bitch wants to test something? Fine. We'll test something. Everyone arm up, and we'll crack out the special toys. We're going to kill whoever shows up and make a real ghost out of her."

The men all cheered, except Andy. He shook his head.

"We're all going to die."

Johnny gestured to Andy. "Get some bandages on him and Vicodin in him and throw him in a back room. We've got shit to do."

Johnny smiled at the glowing *jian* in his hand. He wasn't much of a fan of swords. When he was a kid, he'd always preferred gangster films over *wuxia*. Magic might have returned to the world, but normal men like him could still get ahead through strength of will, bravery and a good gun.

You won't win, Silver Ghost. Not against me. I'm not

running or surrendering to anyone anymore. That shit stops tonight.

The gangsters stood around, double-checking their weapons. Most had handguns, shotguns, or rifles, but a few had enchanted blades like Johnny, and one man even held a thin lightning spear Johnny had been told was made out of dragon bone.

"Listen up," Johnny shouted. "We're still pretty new to LA, which means it's important we deliver a loud and clear message tonight. We'll let everyone know that we're going to keep expanding operations and that anyone who dares fuck with us dies. Generous in peace, ruthless in war."

The men raised their weapons and shouted.

We're not the same triad we were when we first came to LA. We're better and stronger, and we're going to prove it tonight to whatever bitch shows up.

Johnny glanced at a clock on the wall. From what Andy told them, the Silver Ghost should have already arrived.

"No matter what, we make sure that bitch dies here."

A loud thump sounded from a back hallway, and the men all turned that way.

Johnny snorted. "See? If that's the best she's got, this won't take long." He flicked his wrist at a group standing near the entrance to the hallway. "Go kill her, and leave the body there. We'll take it somewhere else to dump it and clean up right away."

A half-dozen men charged into the hallway, weapons at the ready, both men with guns and a few swordsmen.

Loud gunshots echoed through the hallway. A few seconds later, so did screams.

"What the fuck?" Johnny frowned, his heart pounding.

He nodded to the man holding the lightning spear. "Hide behind the bar. Surprise her ass when she least expects it."

The spearman rushed toward the bar and vaulted over it, his face pale.

Fuck. I should have taken the damned spear.

Another scream came from the hallway. The headless body of one of the gangsters flew through the door and crashed into a table. His arm, still clutching a sword, came next.

Several men's eyes widened, and they trembled.

"Don't let her freak you out," Johnny shouted, bile rising in the back of his throat. "Just be pissed that some bitch thought she could come in here and run off the 25K!"

"'Thought,'" came a cold but feminine voice from around the corner, "implies I won't be successful, and you can't be foolish enough to believe that after what you've just seen."

Johnny saw the glint before she turned the corner revealing herself, a lithe female form covered from head to toe in silver skin. Given how closely the silver followed the smooth curves and contours of her body, he wouldn't have been surprised if it was her actual skin except for her featureless face. No eyes, no mouth, nothing; only a blank, smooth, reflective surface.

"What the fuck?" Johnny narrowed his eyes. "You some sort of Oriceran robot?"

The Silver Ghost stopped. Her fingers and forearm flowed like liquid and morphed into a long, flat double-edged blade.

"Neither," she replied. "I applaud your bravery.

Standing firm in the face of certain death is to be respected, even if it is parasites doing it."

Johnny snorted. "Parasites? We're businessmen. We provide services to people, and we don't mess with no one who doesn't have it coming."

"Businessmen? You prey on the weak through force." The Silver Ghost pointed her blade arm at him. "That is why your life is forfeit. All your lives are forfeit."

"Fuck you." Johnny pointed at her with the *jian*. "Kill this Ori bitch."

The roar of dozens of guns going off simultaneously deafened Johnny. The Silver Ghost jerked with each hit, and Johnny's grin grew.

You're nothing when you don't surprise people, are you, bitch? Shouldn't have gotten so damned cocky.

The gangsters kept flinging bullets, kicking up dust, wood, and drywall with the bullets not striking the Silver Ghost.

Triumph swelled in Johnny with each hit, but after ten seconds, his grin faded and a frown replaced it. The Ghost was obviously taking hits, but there was no blood on the walls or floor. He didn't care if it was red, green, silver, pink, or whatever color, but he doubted they could kill someone who wasn't bleeding.

"Just die already," he muttered.

The sustained fire forced the Ghost against a wall, various shallow dark idents in her body, but she didn't collapse, and she refused to bleed.

"Stop firing!" Johnny shouted. "Stop fucking firing!"

Shots continued for a few seconds before trickling off.

The Silver Ghost tilted her head, but it was hard to interpret her body language without a face. "Thank you."

Johnny frowned. "Thank you? Huh?"

"I was confident I'd be able to stand up to that level of attack, but I hadn't actually tested it." The Silver Ghost took a few steps forward. Silver liquid flowed from the edges of the indents, sealing them. "This calibration and testing session has been very useful. Extremely so."

"If you have them, put in your anti-magic bullets," Johnny ordered. He shook his head. "I was hoping not to have to use those, but congrats—you pushed us to this, Ghost. You should be proud, you crazy bitch. I'm going to have to justify this shit later to my bosses."

A few men ejected their magazines and loaded new ones, but the Silver Ghost advanced without apparent concern, her movements slow and deliberate. Even elegant in a way.

"Kill her!" Johnny shouted.

The guns roared again, the Silver Ghost again jerking with the impacts, but this time she continued moving forward.

What the fuck? Those anti-magic bullets should be tearing her up, but I don't even see any holes in her body.

Johnny gripped his sword tightly. Maybe she had some sort of magic that protected her from bullets but wouldn't work against hand-to-hand weapons? He'd heard about that kind of thing.

The Silver Ghost's languid pace switched to a quick sprint forward. She sliced off the head of a man before leaping toward another and impaling him. Her victim coughed up blood, his face a mask of pain and surprise.

No fucking way. This shit isn't happening. I'm not seeing this.

She pulled the blade out and kicked the body toward two nearby gangsters. A man near the hallway door dropped his gun and tried to leave.

The Silver Ghost raised her non-blade arm. Golden circles of light pulsed from the back to the front and discharged as a bright bolt of energy that struck the fleeing man. The attack burned a gaping hole in his back and he fell to the ground, the stench of his burning flesh filling the air.

Johnny watched, mouth agape, his hold slackening on his sword, as the Silver Ghost darted from man to man, stabbing and slicing. Quick energy blasts killed men on the periphery.

A brave few continued to fire, but they weren't hurting her.

The spearman popped up, spotted the carnage, and ducked back down.

"What are you?" Johnny whispered. His blade clattered to the ground and he stumbled forward, his stomach lurching as he took in all the dead men littering the restaurant.

"A blade," the Silver Ghost replied, and kicked a few chairs aside. "A blade of justice. A blade of vengeance. A blade who will never forget those who died at the hands of monsters." She pointed her other arm toward the bar and fired an energy blast. It blasted through the wood, leaving a smoking hole, and the enforcer cowering behind it couldn't even get out a scream before he died, his spear never getting its chance to be used. "I would have left the rest of you parasites to the local authorities, but as I said, I needed additional testing and calibration."

Johnny fell to his knees and shook his head. "I don't get this. We provide services. We don't fuck over people unless they come at us or they disrespect us. We're not like the Harriken. We don't even traffic."

"Oppression and tyranny offer many excuses and evil hides behind many faces. But that's all they are in the end— excuses and disguises." Her head turned. "Ah, I was wondering where you were. This saves me the trouble of tracking you down later."

Johnny looked over his shoulder. Andy stood a few feet behind him, his coat and shirt off and his body covered in bandages. His face twisted in rage, and his eyes bulged. He held the *jian* aloft.

"I'm going to kill you," Andy screamed. "I'm going to show Johnny what kind of man I am. I'm going to redeem myself." He raised the sword and charged the Silver Ghost.

She didn't move, just allowed the gangster to close on her. Once he was a yard away, she lunged forward. Her blade pierced his heart and pushed out his back.

Andy coughed up blood and tried to swing the *jian*, but she caught his wrist with her other hand. She slowly tightened her grip, the crack and snap of each bone audible. The wounded man coughed up more blood and his head lolled forward, his eyes rolling up in the back of his head as he died.

The Silver Ghost removed her blade and let the body drop to the floor. She stepped toward Johnny. "Anything you want to say? Perhaps beg for your life some more? You might persuade me, but I doubt it. I've already learned a lot about you and your friends."

Johnny forced a grin and spat in her face, or at least where a face would be. "You know what? Fuck you. I might have got a little spooked earlier, but real 25K Triad doesn't beg. You may think you're the baddest bitch in LA, but you'll get yours. You're not even like that dark-haired bitch. She was tough, but you're a monster, and monsters always have other monsters swallow them in the end. Just ask the Eyes. Oh, you can't, because Brownstone fucking killed him."

"Brownstone?" The Silver Ghost chuckled. "Yes, Brownstone. Let me worry about him." The Silver Ghost raised her blade. "I applaud you for not fleeing. A commander who leaves his men is the worst sort of coward."

Johnny closed his eyes. "Just do it."

"Very well."

The pain lasted only the briefest of seconds as she separated his head from his body.

CHAPTER FOUR

Weber took a few deep breaths as he stepped into the briefing room, the gathered men and women of AET already sitting behind the tables. This would be his first brief as a newly-promoted lieutenant, and he didn't want to screw it up.

Maria left some big boots to fill, but I can do this.

The murmuring and crosstalk died down when he came in. The cool gazes of his fellow officers focused on him, waiting.

He headed over to the podium and stood behind it, placing his hands on the sides. "Sorry to bring you all in so suddenly, but word's come down from on high about a new priority. Our top deployment priority, in fact. I wanted to bring everyone up to speed in person so you can ask any questions you might have."

Everyone stared at him, their faces set in grim determination. They probably already knew what he was about to say.

Good, that should make this easier.

Weber took a deep breath. "Three hours ago, based on some eyewitness reports, the vigilante known as the Silver Ghost slaughtered almost all known members of the 25K Triad currently in LA at Kowloon, their restaurant. There are a handful of members who weren't present at the incident site, but from what we've heard, those men have already fled LA and are probably on their way to San Francisco. Initial witness statements suggest that the 25K men knew she was coming, and judging by the quantity and type of weapons found on site, along with the huge pile of bullets and bullet casings, and including several magical artifacts, they put up a good fight."

Murmurs broke out, and Weber waited a few seconds for the room to quiet.

He frowned. "The successful apprehension of the Silver Ghost is now the top priority of the entire LAPD, and a wide variety of resources and assets are being tasked for this mission, including surveillance drones, and, well, *us*. The mayor and the chief want her captured ASAP, and they figure the AET will have to be the one to bring her in or take her down if she refuses to come in. Since no police officers have had contact with her, we can't be sure how she'll react to police commands."

Sergeant McMahon, who sat at one of the front tables, shook his head. "Look, the 25K weren't as bad as, say, the Harriken were, but they weren't exactly a bunch of choir boys, either. I know we have to do our job, but I don't get why the brass are so concerned about some crazy Oriceran chick cleaning up a little. She's probably some fresh-out-of-the portal type who doesn't get our laws. Once someone explains it to her, she'll calm down. We devote a bunch of resources to this one woman, and we'll end up with trouble elsewhere."

Several other officers nodded their agreement.

Weber cleared his throat. "This is pure vigilantism, and you don't have to be Maria to think it might have a bad effect on the city. The chief is worried that things are already spiraling out of control. Before, the Ghost was taking out a target or two here and there, but killing dozens of men threatens to, in the chief's words, 'destabilize everything.' She's upped her game in a big way, and there's no reason to think she won't escalate even more."

Jacobs frowned. "But violent crime's been going down steadily this year. I get that this messes with our stats, but things are still under control. The brass should change their diapers and calm down. One Oriceran vigilantewoman isn't going to cause riots all across the city."

Weber shrugged. "Maybe, but we need to be real about the reasons for crime decreasing. AET and the rest of the LAPD have been doing a good job, but we all know the reason high-level violent crime is down is that everyone's afraid of getting James Brownstone's attention. Just when thugs think it's okay to stir up shit, he throws those robbers through a pet store window and then everyone remembers what they're risking. Criminals know that if they keep a low profile and don't make noise, they probably won't have to deal with Brownstone, but the Silver Ghost is changing the equation. She's making it seem like no matter what you do, she'll come after you and kill you, even if you don't have much of a rep."

"Why not send Brownstone?"

"There's no current bounty, so he's not going to move

on her, and the chief doesn't want a bounty issued on her if we can bring her in ourselves."

A cop in the middle frowned and shook her head. "This 25K thing isn't half as bad as crap like the Council attack or that witch at the farmer's market. Hell, what about Brownstone killing the Harriken? The LAPD set up a security perimeter for him when he went in the one time. And Hall might have had a hard-on for going after him, but in the end, she started working for him, and our captain and the chief both have made it clear they don't want us messing much with him. So why do they care so much about the Silver Ghost?"

"Not the same thing," Weber replied, gripping the sides of the podium tightly. "Brownstone's a bounty hunter, so at least he plays within the system somewhat. He also respects and listens to cops, and I'm not just talking about the donuts and donations. Remember how he coordinated things with the LAPD when he was leading the hitmen out of the city?" He released the podium. "Brownstone may make a mess, but he cares about staying on good terms with us. Not only that, it's like you said—Maria works for him now, and Sergeant Mack's his friend. They can always whisper in his ear and push him away from something that's going to cause too much trouble. I don't think of him as a vigilante or even a bounty hunter. I think of him as backup we can call on if things get too tough. It just so happens he's not an immediate option in this case."

Jacobs crossed his arms. "How do we know the Silver Ghost doesn't like cops? The 25K might have brought this thing on themselves. Maybe they crossed a line they shouldn't have or something like that. Plenty of cops in the city she could go after if she was just an Oriceran on a power trip."

"We don't know one way or another, but we can't ignore the pattern." Weber shrugged. "She hasn't killed any non-criminal targets yet, but she also hasn't killed an entire roomful of men before. And we're not just talking about shooting a few guys. Decapitations, stabbings, guys with holes burned through them." He sucked in a breath. "It was pretty nasty."

"Lots of deaths are brutal. We've all seen what a railgun can do to a man." McMahon frowned. "Besides, this is really just about the brass covering their ass. That's why they suddenly care about this escalation, and that's why they won't issue a bounty. They forced the department to bury the recent vigilante cases, and now it's going to look like a cover-up. They're probably looking for scapegoats."

Several other AET officers nodded their agreement, frowns on their faces.

"Not going to say the same thing hasn't occurred to me," Weber replied, "but from what the chief has passed on to me, some of the other units are seeing bad signs, so this isn't just politics and CYA anymore. It's a serious threat to public safety, and AET needs to be at the forefront of dealing with it."

"Bad signs?" McMahon frowned. "What the hell does that mean?"

"Look, it's an escalation thing, right?" Weber gestured toward a window. "At least Brownstone is a known factor, and like I said, even the criminals get that he's not going to wander around LA killing any random criminal he runs into, but there's already a lot of chatter from informants about how the underworld is treating the Silver Ghost differently from the Granite Ghost."

"How so?"

"A lot of gangs and organized crime groups are worried about the Silver Ghost, including normal and enhanced threats. There's talk of arming up, maybe doing joint patrols, even forming alliances until she's dead." Weber frowned. "The last thing we need is a lot of these assholes deciding they should work together and sending armed posses around town. Imagine what would happen if say the Russian Mafia teamed up with the Yakuza." He shook his head. "They're going to end up hurting innocent people or maybe convince other enhanced individuals to proactively go after criminals. Next thing you know, LA's on fire and a damned war zone. Things could get as bad as they did when the gates first started opening. The fact we still have so many bounty hunters should be proof enough that we don't want to go back to that."

The gathered cops all nodded, determined looks on their faces as they murmured their agreement.

Weber summoned his inner Hall and glared at the officers in front of him. "This is a briefing, not a debate. The orders have come down: we're to stay on maximum standby with at least two teams ready to deploy 24/7 until the Silver Ghost has either been determined to have permanently left town or we've caught her. Understood?"

"Understood," the cops replied in unison.

Weber swept the room with a steely gaze. "Ladies and gentlemen, we'll catch the Silver Ghost before it's too late and let every wannabe vigilante in LA know that the LAPD is still the Thin Blue Line protecting this city."

CHAPTER FIVE

James frowned as he took a seat across from Anna. A green silk tablecloth covered the table, and there was an elaborate floral centerpiece. There were also way too many forks and spoons of different sizes. Another expensive and complicated restaurant—the kind Shay liked to make him go to every now and again.

All this decoration shit just detracts from the food.

Anna offered him a polite nod. The last time he'd seen the Celtic faerie she'd gone with a professional look, but today the pale blonde wore a clinging gray metallic strapless high-slit dress and lethal-looking heels. Her glasses were gone, and her hair was loose except for two small braids. She rested her red eyes on him with a faint smile.

"Hey, Anna," he rumbled.

Anna propped her elbow on the table and her cheek in her palm, her creamy neck on full display. "Good afternoon, Mr. Brownstone. I've already taken the liberty of ordering. I've heard the tuna *crudo* here is divine, and I'm sure you'd enjoy it given a chance. Everything I know about you, after all, suggests you're a man who enjoys eating.

"I enjoy some stuff." James blinked and frowned, having trouble concentrating just like the first time he'd met her. He shook his head to clear it. No Celtic succubus was going to pull him off his Shay-centered mission. "Can you shut the sexy aura or whatever off?"

Anna let out a quiet laugh. "It's an inherent part of what I am. Is it really so distracting?"

"More annoying than distracting." James gestured toward her dress. "And what's with the outfit? I thought you were going for the whole sexy librarian thing rather than 'woman going to a cocktail party.'"

"My body and sartorial choices are a type of art in and of themselves, and it's important to change myself so I can become the most effective muse to my current artist." Anna smiled and lifted her head. "The man I provide inspiration for now is less moved by, as you say, 'sexy librarians.'"

James grunted. "Oh. That makes sense, I guess. Whatever works."

"I'm glad you understand. And what about you, hmm? Last time we spoke, I believe you mentioned a particularly jealous girlfriend with magic knives?" Anna raised a pale eyebrow. "Or have you moved on to a less lethal woman? Somehow I doubt it. The woman who could capture your heart will, by her very nature, probably be just as dangerous as you are."

James nodded. "That's why I'm here, actually. I want advice. Same woman, and she needs a special proposal. I need advice on how to deliver one. I figure you've lived a long time and think about a lot of romance shit, so maybe you could help."

Anna smiled softly. "How wonderful. Despite what you might think, I find myself envious of those who can commit to another for a lifetime. It's something I will never be able to truly do for many reasons, most outside my control." Sadness flickered across her face for a moment before she pushed it away with an obviously forced smile. "Before we continue, let me ask you something. Did the discussions we had for the Bard of Filth competition give you any insight into sexuality and people's interface with it? I'm assuming they did, or you wouldn't have had a chance. Humor requires deep insight into the human condition. It's one of the reasons I found myself drawn to comedic artists. The good ones have such a fascinating understanding of the world."

James looked around with a frown. "Yeah. I guess those discussions helped. I didn't win, but I came in second, and the shit did involve sex and the woman I want to marry. I finally understood why people find sex jokes funny, so that's got to mean something, right?"

"Delightful. I'm glad our talk was of assistance." Anna picked up her glass of wine and took a small sip. "Unfortunately, if that's the case, I suspect there's little I can do to help you in this matter, Mr. Brownstone."

James grimaced and was about to say something when the waiter arrived and set plates in front of them. Both held sliced tuna *crudo* covered in capers and red pepper flakes. After a polite nod, the waiter departed.

The bounty hunter frowned down at the meal in front

of him, not bothering to hide his disdain. "This doesn't even look like it's been cooked."

"That's kind of the point of *crudo*." Anna let out a quiet chuckle. "Cooking isn't necessary for every grand meal, Mr. Brownstone."

"My daughter made me go to a sushi place last time she was in town." James made a face. "I think she's getting a taste for it, but I prefer my meat cooked. I'm a barbeque guy, and it's all about cooking."

Anna squeezed a few drops of lemon on top of some tuna and took a bite, inhaling and letting out a quiet murmur of appreciation. "You're really missing out." She winked. "And you're paying. More's the pity."

James waved a hand. "That's okay. I think I'll stop by In-N-Out on my way home for a Quad-Quad." He didn't want wine or raw fish, but a little water wouldn't hurt. He picked up his glass and took a sip, relieved that it tasted like nothing besides cold water.

This is okay, and at least it's not some weird health water. How do people manage to make even water complicated?

Anna swallowed and set her fork down. "But back to our previous discussion. I'm assuming you've come to me because you're desperate. You've perhaps talked to many different people, and you found you're no closer to the perfect plan than you were before."

James grunted. "Exactly. I get that you're focused on a particular kind of guy, but you have to know about romance and shit. I'm sure you can help me plan something."

Anna clucked her tongue. "That's where you're already going wrong."

"Huh?"

She reached over and patted his hand. He snatched it back, half-worried about leanan sidhe seduction. Anna's face suggested she was more amused than annoyed.

"There are different beliefs, of course, but I'm of the belief that the purest expressions of romance are without calculation," Anna offered quietly, her voice a near-whisper. "Planning and artifice are antithetical to such pure expressions of emotion. The thing is, you already know what you need to do if you've gotten to the point of wanting to marry the woman. You're letting your brain distract your heart."

"But I *don't* know, and she says it has to be fucking epic. I tried before, but she cut me off. I didn't even have the ring then, but I do now—and it's epic, too—but I still don't know what to do."

"Fucking epic?" Anna laughed. "How adorable. Still, that changes nothing. The truly effective connections and gestures come from spontaneity and not the artifice of careful and scripted planning. The very act of planning the gesture may smother the romance under logistics and cold rationality. Men, prone to over-planning to begin with, often tend to have extreme problems with this."

James furrowed his brow. "So, you're saying there's no perfect proposal?"

Anna shook her head, her red eyes alight with amusement. "No, no—quite the opposite. There's of course a perfect proposal for all who wish to pledge themselves to one another, depending on circumstance. I'm simply arguing that you might not be able to find it if you're busy attempting to force it into being. Let me ask you...

When you started to ask her before, did you have a big plan?"

"No. It just felt right."

"Then remember that feeling." Anna took another sip of her wine. "It sounds like you had the right idea before, but maybe she wasn't ready. Now you have a ring and a burning desire to be with her, so it's simply a matter of waiting for the right place and the right time. Stop thinking about it, and it'll naturally present itself."

"That's not what they said on the podcasts."

"Unless any of those podcasters are as old as I am, I'm willing to bet I've had more practical and direct experience with that sort of thing." Anna took another bite of her *crudo* with a smile.

"So wait for the right moment, then just do it. No fancy planning, no skywriting, no Jumbotron at the stadium?"

"I don't even need to know the woman to know that anyone who could choose you wouldn't be impressed by skywriting or other such banal efforts." Anna sighed. "The right moment hasn't arisen because you've been too preoccupied with trying to bring it about. I guarantee you that if you stop thinking so hard about it, you'll probably be able to propose to her in a matter of weeks, if not days. If you're still having trouble in a couple of weeks, call me again and we can discuss the problem some more. Do make sure you always have the engagement ring with you, though. You don't want a chance to pass you by."

Will that shit actually work? Don't know, but at least she's saying I can come back. Maybe it will help just to not think about it so much.

James nodded. "Okay, fair enough, then." He shrugged.

"That's my end of things, but it sounded like you wanted me for something when I called."

Anna's smile faded, and her mouth twisted into a frown, which didn't suit her pretty face. "Yes, I wanted to call in my favor. As you can imagine, a being such as me can sometimes find herself the center of unwanted attention. Through no efforts of my own, I've acquired a stalker." She sighed and shook her head. "I'm not asking you for anything as barbaric as killing him, but I do think the appearance of the famous James Brownstone might be enough in and of itself to dissuade this man from pursuing me further."

"Why haven't you gone to the cops?"

She shrugged. "I don't trust human authorities. Consider it holding a grudge, but far too many tried to murder me or burn me in more primitive times, and because of what I am, I've even had trouble in modern times with human authorities convinced I'm purposely charming men with my abilities, so they ignore my criminal complaints."

Chasing off a stalker? That shit sounds easy enough.

"I'm listening." James cracked his knuckles. "Who is this asshole?"

"He goes by Fifty-six."

"Huh?"

"That's his chosen name—Fifty-six." Anna sighed. "He's rather pretentious. He's a musician and a wizard who fancies himself as pushing the boundaries of artistry with his magic and sound efforts. That's where I come in. I met him briefly at a party a few weeks ago, and he's become obsessed with the idea of a leanan sidhe being the source of inspiration to take his art to the next level."

James shrugged. "And you're not interested in this guy at all?"

Anna snorted. "No, he's a boring and shallow individual who produces trite art masquerading as radical. My inspiration would be wasted on a man like him, and I don't like the idea that he thinks he can force me into serving as his muse."

"Couldn't you just agree and then drain him until he's dry? Just saying."

"I have certain rules I live by. I prefer not to violate them even for annoying men." Anna traced her finger around the rim of her wine glass. "And he hasn't done enough to warrant death. I find violence unpleasant."

James grunted. "If I'm involved, things might end up violent."

"I hope that you being who you are will prevent that." Anna smiled at James. "Is this something you can help me with, Mr. Brownstone? I did help you with your little contest, and I guarantee that my advice will be helpful for you and your beloved."

"Fine, but I don't want to have to go running halfway around the city looking for this asshole."

"Not a problem," Anna replied. "Despite his lifestyle of Bohemian wandering, he's invited me to a performance at a club in a few days. I figure that will be a good spot for you to confront him, even if I'm not present. I will send you the date and time."

James nodded. "Sounds good, but to be clear, unless this

asshole has a bounty, I'm just going to have a loud conversation with him."

"That's all I ask." Anna picked up her fork. "You really should try the *crudo*. You're missing out."

"I'm okay with missing out on some shit."

CHAPTER SIX

Trey sidled up to the bar, Zoe in tow and a smile plastered on his face. He surveyed the room, taking in everything: the tablecloths, soft lighting, and light jazz playing from the speakers. There wasn't a tv in the place, and several impressionist paintings hung on the walls.

Place is more rocking a gastropub vibe than a bar. Classy. Glad I'm in my suit.

The bartender turned toward him—an attractive brunette in a silk shirt and dark vest. It was Kathy, co-owner and former Black Sun employee.

"How do you like the White Sun?" she asked with a smile. "This is your first time here since we opened. I was beginning to think you were avoiding the place, Trey."

"Nah, just how the schedules worked out." Trey shrugged. "It's definitely got a fancier vibe than Tyler's place, that's for sure. Several of the boys who have already been here had good things to say, but I had to see it myself to make up my mind. Lachlan don't like it, but he ain't got no taste, so don't mind that little bitch."

Kathy chuckled. "He's not the only one. When Brownstone came, he was annoyed we didn't have ribs for him. I did satisfy him with Irish Stout on tap, but he kept mumbling under his breath about that Irish pub he hangs out at."

"That's the big man for you. He's got what he likes, and it hasn't much changed, I suspect, for a long time." Trey laughed. "He's like a mountain who just happens to be a man."

Kathy snorted. "That's the best description I've heard of him yet."

Trey nodded toward Zoe. "This is my girlfriend, Zoe."

Kathy extended her hand. "I've heard a lot of about you."

Zoe shook the hand with a soft smile. "And me you. Congratulations on your business successes."

"Thanks."

"But ain't you worried this'll scare off the scumbags?" Trey frowned and looked around. Almost everyone in the room wore a nice dress or suit, and most of the men sported ties. There were none of the gangbanger scum or obvious bruiser thugs he might see at the Black Sun back in LA.

"What are you talking about?" Kathy frowned

Trey shrugged. "The fancy and classy atmosphere. No Demon General would come into a place like this. Yeah, I know there ain't no Demon Generals in Vegas, just using them as an example."

Zoe gave Kathy a pleasant smile and folded her hands in front of her, a curious look on her face.

"Not worried about that. If anything, it's an advantage

of this place." Kathy shook her head. "Tyler spent too much time with bottom feeders. That was why it took him so long to crawl out of the bottom, and he needed Brownstone's help." She placed her hand on her chest. "I'd rather cultivate contacts with the strivers and the top guys, and they can feed me information from the gutter rats. You don't have to roll in the sewer to smell it."

Trey and Zoe laughed.

"So what can I get for you two? This *is* a bar, after all." Kathy looked at Zoe and Trey.

Zoe licked her lips, her gaze roaming the bottles with hungry desire. It'd been a whole half a day since she had last drunk any alcohol. "A pear martini."

Trey scratched his chin. "I'll have a Manhattan."

Kathy nodded. "Coming right up." She turned to grab the glasses and necessary bottles.

Trey turned to Zoe. "You sure about coming to Vegas with me on this trip? I mean, I'm working as part of my agency rotation. Not gonna have much time for fun, you know what I'm saying? I'm gonna have to hit the streets a lot with the boys and Victoria to hunt down bounties."

The witch smiled and turned to take in the ambiance of the bar. "I've rarely left Los Angeles in recent decades, and it's important to go to a place to truly appreciate the atmosphere there. Since you're considering moving here, don't you think that's a good idea? I can travel around the city and take in the sights without you at my side, at least for a day or two."

"I'm just thinking about moving. I ain't made up my mind." Trey shrugged.

"Still, the possibility is there."

"Yeah, I guess." Trey considered that for a moment. "Just maybe figured I could take some days off and we could do it that way, rather than me half-assing it after work, but if *you* don't care, I don't." He gestured around. "This place is part of work, you know. Kathy passes shit to us we need to know for a price, and we make it clear that people don't come and bust this place up without repercussions, but at the same time, we make it clear this is just like Black Sun: neutral ground. The Vegas cops ain't happy about it, but they've said that if we take responsibility, they ain't going to go out of their way to send cops in here."

Zoe gave him a tight grin. "I'm sure after what happened to that barbeque thief, people are loath to cross the Brownstone Agency."

Kathy finished preparing the drinks and set them down in front of Zoe and Trey. "That's the idea, anyway. It hasn't been tested. Still worried about the cops respecting the neutrality. A few come in, but it's not like it was in LA, where tons of cops were in the Black Sun all the time. I don't know if that's a good thing or a bad one."

Trey shrugged. "Give it time, maybe?"

Zoe's gray eyes surveyed the customers sitting at the tables. "Far be it from me to tell either of you how to deal with less than reputable people, but isn't it an advantage to not have so many police here? Neutrality or not, I doubt that criminals will truly be comfortable and willing to pass along information if there are police around them."

A few more customers sat down at the other end of the bar. Kathy nodded to Zoe and Trey and headed over to serve them.

A man in a gray suit with gold chains around his neck

sat down at the bar just a few feet from Trey. He looked at the bounty hunter with a frown, and his eyes widened.

Trey resisted a smirk. He'd seen the man's picture on his bounty hunting app that morning—John something-or-other. He couldn't remember the name, but this was as good as time as any to reinforce the neutrality of the White Sun with the imprimatur of the Brownstone Agency.

"Problem?" Trey took a sip of his drink. "Because I ain't here for a problem. I'm just here for this sweet-ass Manhattan."

Zoe sipped her drink, watching in silence. There was no concern on her face.

She ain't ever really seen me in action. This will be a nice show.

The man took a deep breath. "You're Trey Garfield with the Brownstone Agency."

"Yeah." Trey shrugged. "Last time I checked, I was. You heard different? Because if you have, I'd really like to know who is saying that shit so I could correct them, you know what I'm saying?"

The man looked him up and down. "But you don't know who I am?"

"Oh, yeah, I know who you are, John. Level one bounty, and all that shit." Trey shrugged. "Just don't care." He held up his glass. "Right now, the only thing I give a shit about is this drink." He nodded at Zoe. "And this fine-ass woman here. That clear enough for you?"

Confusion rather than relief appeared on John's face. "You not going after ones anymore? I haven't heard anything about the Brownstone Agency passing on low-level bounties, even if Brownstone does."

Trey shook his head. "Nope, we don't pass on low-level bounties."

John tensed, his hands inching toward his jacket.

Trey snorted. "Don't be a dumbass motherfucker, John. If I wanted to bust your ass and drag you in, don't you think I would have done it already?"

Several nearby patrons turned to watch the commotion. Kathy turned and watched, a slight frown on her face.

The other man's hand stopped moving and he furrowed his brow. "I don't get it. You just said you're not giving up on low-level bounties."

"On the streets, yeah." Trey took another sip of his drink and sighed. "But this is the White Sun. Haven't you heard the deal?"

John's gaze darted between Trey and the exit. "The word on the street is that this place is neutral ground, but some people are saying that's just a trick. A trap that you all set up."

Trey snorted. "What kind of dust-addled plan would that be? It'd only work once. Nah, that shit is real. This is neutral ground. Rules are simple: you come in and drink and don't cause no problems, you don't get no problems while you're here. Building and parking lot are off-limits." His expression darkened. "But you break those rules, we'll have all sorts of trouble. Then we have to go and talk to you like we talked to Demetrius. You heard of him?"

John licked his lips. "He robbed Jessie Rae's, which is the official barbeque place of the Brownstone Agency or some shit like that."

"Exactly." Trey smiled. "Consider this the official bar of

our agency, except we want to make sure everyone can enjoy it, so we enforce neutrality."

"Fine, I believe you, but can I go sit at a table? Sitting next to a Brownstone bounty hunter is making me nervous."

Trey nodded toward an empty table. "Be my guest."

John hopped off his stool and hurried over to the table, checking over his shoulder every few steps.

Zoe polished off the last of her martini, her cheeks red. "It's interesting to see how much they fear you."

Trey shrugged. "It's more the big man they fear."

Zoe shook her head. "No, it's you. You've become a burning fire, but one that isn't raging out of control like James. It's fascinating." She gestured around the dimly lit room. "But seeing that interaction and listening to your discussion with Kathy makes some things clear to me."

"Like what?"

"You have no choice." Zoe shook her head. "Kathy said it herself. The police aren't providing the protection for this place, the agency is, and James is rarely in Las Vegas. The next most powerful bounty hunters have to be viable threats or some enemy will eventually think the neutrality doesn't apply to them."

Trey grinned. "It ain't no thing. I'm here a lot."

"Not enough." Zoe picked up her drink and upended it so she could lick off the last few stray drops of alcohol. "Second-order fear won't work. You'll need to have a permanent presence here, not merely rotating members. Since James can't be here, you at least will need to come. If criminals know that you and Victoria are always available to respond to threats, they'll be less inclined to violate the neutrality you're attempting to enforce."

Trey stopped grinning. "You're saying I should move here then, straight up? You ain't even seen much. How much vibe could you have gotten?"

"Don't worry about me. I'm like a hardy weed. I will grow anywhere, provided I have enough…sustenance. If you wish to come here, I will accompany you." Zoe stared at him with a heavy-lidded gaze. "Everything is pulling you to this city, and I think you should strongly consider not fighting the winds pushing you."

Trey finished his Manhattan and blew out a breath. "It's tempting, you know? Been thinking about it a lot. It's not even like I have to leave all my boys behind if some them keep doing rotations up here, but there's Auntie Charlyce and Nana to consider."

Zoe nodded. "Family is important, but I imagine your family wants you to do what's best for you."

"Yeah, but I ain't making no decision like this without talking to Nana first. I owe her that much."

"Of course. I think that's a good idea."

Is she really okay with this?

Trey looked Zoe up and down. Other than her rosy cheeks, she didn't look that drunk, and considering how much alcohol she normally consumed, he doubted one martini was enough to seriously affect her mind. Whatever she was saying wasn't coming from a place of drunkenness, and even if it were, he wasn't sure that mattered when it came to a witch following the Dionysian Way. Half her power came from alcohol.

"And you're sure?" Trey furrowed his brow.

Zoe let out a merry giggle. "You misunderstand me. Of course, I'm not sure."

Trey frowned. "Then why are you pushing me so hard?"

Zoe reached up to brush her soft hand over his cheek. "Because I don't need to be sure, my little supernova. When you live as long as I have, you learn to simply flow with life. For now, that's you. Talk to your grandmother and any friends you think are important, but right now I need another martini." She raised her hand and smiled at Kathy, who was at the other end of the bar.

Shit. It does sound good, becoming Vegas Trey. Maybe I should change my wardrobe. Nah. Classic dark suit works, whatever city you're in.

CHAPTER SEVEN

Clad in only his boxers, James finished filling Thomas' food and water bowls before shutting off the kitchen light and making his way to the basement door. He tapped in the code on the keypad and placed his thumb on the DNA scanner.

Once the door had clicked open, he headed down the stairs and over to the shelves filled with different boxes—ammo, weapons, and grenades, more than enough to defend himself if he needed to, along with various tools of the trade. Anything he couldn't get there, he could get from Shay's Warehouse Three. Maintaining his own external storage seemed pointless these days, especially after he started keeping his amulet on him all the time at Alison's insistence.

At some point, I stopped thinking of our shit as separate. The future's waiting for us. We just have to find the right path to get there.

Even though his enemies' strength and numbers had grown, James worried less about the future now, if only because he'd learned to better control his amulet and unlock his power. It didn't matter what he was meant to be on his home planet. What mattered was what he'd chosen to be. The symbiont didn't rule him; he ruled the symbiont, even when he was pissed.

The Church was still working out the theological implications of so many different intelligent species, and they were only concerned with Oriceran, let alone other planets. James was a simple man, though, so he'd let others figure that shit out. For now, all he'd worry about was protecting what was important to him.

If people threatened him, he'd take them out. If they left him and his people alone, they might live.

Erin or whatever the hell her real name was might still be out there, but until she decided to come at him again, he wasn't going to worry about her. An enemy who had to hide from him was an enemy who feared him, and an enemy who feared him was one he could defeat.

What are you doing right now? Trying to scheme how to get back to your home planet because you think I'm the Space Bogeyman?

James let out a low growl. Where were Erin and her advanced technology when the Council was killing people, or when he was taking down any of the dangerous magical killers native to Earth?

You better never show your face to me again, or I'll make you pay for sending people at Shay and me.

James headed back up the stairs and closed the reinforced basement door behind him. After the keypad beeped and the lock clicked, he headed into the hallway toward his bedroom.

When he stepped inside, his gaze shifted to his amulet on the nightstand—his blessing and his curse.

If I didn't have Whispy, that bitch probably wouldn't have come after me, but I wouldn't have been able to kick all the ass I've needed to. I wouldn't have been able to protect Alison from the Drow.

James grunted. For years he'd shunned the amulet, thinking it infernal. It wasn't demonic, however, but the twisted technology of a race who lived in fear and thought it made them strong.

He shook his head and walked toward the bed.

Shay was already under the covers, looking at her phone and mumbling something under her breath.

She glanced up with a grin. "I've gotten ten messages from my department head since that meeting. Mostly they are just forwards of hatchet-job articles on other local universities. I just keep responding with dollar sign emojis and terse little messages like, 'No tenure track, no Shay.'"

James headed to the other side of the bed. "I'm sure it's complicated and shit, but couldn't you just establish some fake foundation or something and pay yourself through grants? Then he wouldn't care about the money, and he wouldn't have to worry about funding."

"Nah, screw that. I'm not paying myself for the privilege of working there." Shay shook her head. "Besides, I like seeing the asshole sweat a little. There's a principle at stake here, and a matter of respect. I'm making him show me respect."

"Whatever you want to do, I'll support you." James shrugged. "Just want you to be happy."

Maybe this would be a good time to practice being spontaneous.

"Hey," James rumbled. "Want to go see a musician wizard? It'd be in a few days."

Shay set her phone on the nightstand and stared at him. "Wait, you mean like a concert? Are you seriously asking me to go to a concert?"

"It's more a performance. I don't know if you'd call it a concert." James shrugged. "Don't know much about the guy other than he uses magic in his music, and that he's a pretentious douchebag. I'm sure his music is shitty."

Shay laughed. "You're really selling this date hard, aren't you? And you don't even like music. You spend all that time listening to podcasts but no music, and suddenly you want to take me on a date to some pretentious douchebag's concert? And you say his music will probably be shitty? You really need to work on your pitches."

"Oh, well, I kind of have to go there anyway, so I figured, you know, I could double shit up. His-and-hers without the ass-kicking. Trying to mix things up, too. Can't always go to a fancy restaurant or a barbeque place." James shrugged. "Who knows? Maybe I'll end up liking this kind of thing."

Shay frowned. "Wait. Why do you have to go see some random wizard musician anyway? Especially one who performs shitty music?"

James took a deep breath. Spontaneity for his actual proposal might be harmed if Shay understood just how much effort he'd put into trying to figure one out and the fact he was recruiting outside help to aid him. He would need to choose his words carefully.

"Remember Anna Forsythe?"

Shay blinked. "That faerie chick who helped you train for the Bard of Filth competition? The leanan sidhe?"

James nodded. "Yeah, her."

"What about her?" Shay sat up. "I'm very interested in how we got from a random date featuring shitty music to a leanan sidhe."

"She's calling in the favor I owe her for her help with the Bard of Filth competition. This musician-wizard douchebag, the guy we're going to see, is stalking her, and she thinks I can help." James shrugged. "I'm not gonna kill him, just have a talk with him and make it clear to him that he needs to leave her the fuck alone. Well, I won't kill him unless he tries something stupid. Then it isn't my fault."

"Wizard stalker?" Shay winced. "I know what that feels like if you count Snegurka. Anna might be better served by you just killing the guy. We both know problems like this don't tend to go away on their own, even after a bloody nose."

"She made it clear she doesn't want that." James shrugged. "And until he has a bounty, I can't just do whatever I want to him without pissing off the cops. I mean, he's a pretentious douchebag who calls himself Fifty-six, so how tough can he be? I'm sure if I just show up and growl at him, he'll run to another state."

Shay rubbed her hands together, a huge grin on her face. "When you first mentioned this idea, I wasn't sure I was all that interested, but now I potentially get to see some asshole stalker-wizard get beat down. I'm liking this idea a lot." She winked. "Also liking your efficiency. It shows you can pull off complicated without even trying that hard, despite how much you like to complain about it."

"Efficiency?" James frowned. "What are you talking about?"

Shay nodded. "You're combining a date with paying back your favor to a magical being. That's efficient. Just like our his-and-hers ass-kicking adventures this year." She shook her finger. "Just so you know, I'm staying out of this shit. The last thing I need is some weird police report making it back to my department head when I'm leaning on him about the position. Then I will have to switch universities, and all the time I put in there will have been wasted."

James nodded. "Fine by me. I'm sure I'll just frown at this guy and he'll piss himself, and it won't be a big deal. If anything happens, I'll handle it. Can't be many people surprised when James Brownstone kicks ass, and your department head is already afraid of me, so he can't get much more afraid."

"It's a date then, with optional ass-kicking." Shay laid back down. "The best kind of date there is."

Trey tied his robe, grabbed his phone from the nightstand, and stepped away from the hotel bed where Zoe still slumbered quietly. Between too many drinks and a little recharging fun for her, they'd had a late night.

He would need to hit the streets that afternoon after rendezvousing with some of the boys at the loft, but he had time to relax in the morning. There was no point in waking Zoe up until he took care of a few things.

He exited the suite's bedroom and walked toward the deck. He opened the door and stepped outside.

Trey looked down at his phone. Nana was an early riser. If he called her, it shouldn't be a problem.

Do I really want to move here? Zoe makes a good point, and something about it feels really right. And I thought it was a big deal when I finally moved out of Nana's house!

The bounty hunter chuckled and shook his head. After everything he'd been through, from leading a gang to helping fight the Council, moving shouldn't be a big deal, but it felt more permanent than anything else he'd done.

Trey shook his head and dialed. Thinking too much had its place, but sometimes a man just had to trust his instincts. He'd promised Shorty he'd live enough life for both of them, and it was time to keep that promise.

"You're calling awfully early," his grandmother answered. "I worry every time you go to Las Vegas because Mr. Brownstone isn't there to back you up most of the time. With him there, I know the bad men will always get taken care of, but I can't be sure when it's just you."

"Nana, we don't be dealing with the crazy level fives and guys like that. The people me and the boys handle don't need Brownstone-level power." Trey chuckled.

Considering he'd been going after level fours lately that wasn't totally true, but there was no reason to worry her over every minor detail of his new career.

"Well, what are you calling me about, Trey?" she responded. "You never call me this early. I was worried that you were calling from the hospital."

"Nah, I'm calling from a hotel. Nice view of the city. I should bring you here sometime."

"I have no reason to go to a place like Las Vegas," his grandmother replied. "No, Trey, I'm fine staying in Los Angeles. What would I even do in Las Vegas? Mr. Brownstone liking that barbeque place isn't enough reason for me to go."

"Just saying, Nana." Trey smiled.

"So if you're not hurt, why are you calling?"

Trey sighed. "I just wanted to talk to you about Vegas. You know I mentioned to you a while back that I was thinking about maybe moving here, mostly to help anchor the Brownstone Agency but also to kind of take the next step in my life."

"Yeah, what about it?" His grandmother clucked her tongue. "I'd say something about it being Sin City, but if it's Sin City, then Los Angeles is the Sin Kingdom. So much has changed since I was a young woman that I don't rightly know how to make sense of the world half the time. Magic, and another planet. It kind of makes my head spin still thinking about it, even though you work with all sorts of magical folks and Mr. Brownstone has his magical armor. Me and Charlyce think it's blessed, you know."

Trey laughed. "The big man's pretty impressive, but I don't know about him being blessed. He's just the biggest badass in LA."

"For all his money and trouble, Mr. Brownstone still goes to church; just keep that in mind. The Lord looks after his own." Nana sniffed.

Trey smiled and stared at the fake Eiffel Tower dominating his field of view.

Is it any less real because it's not the original? This is a city where people used to come to live out fantasies, but the rest of the world's caught up with that now. Maybe it's a good place for a former gang leader and a witch to start over without leaving everyone and everything behind.

"Anyway, Nana, I think I should move here after all," Trey explained. "I mean, I'd come back and visit LA, but it wouldn't just be rotations anymore. I'd be here most of the time. I just wanted to make sure that was okay with you, because I owe you as much as I owe James. He gave me a job, but you gave me hope when I didn't have my own mama to depend on. I don't want you to feel like I'm leaving you behind. You don't deserve that."

"Hush now, Trey," his grandmother replied. "I always knew you'd grow into a fine man if given the chance, and you have, with Mr. Brownstone's help. I also knew that someday you'd need to leave and follow your own path, so I've been ready for this for years. I'm not much worried about you moving to Vegas. It's like you said—you're only a few hours away. You don't worry about your auntie or me, now. You do what's right for you, Trey. You've earned it."

"Thanks, Nana." Trey smiled. "That's all I needed to hear."

CHAPTER EIGHT

James sipped his beer at a small table in the club. The red and white checkerboard vinyl tablecloths were far from the style and level of expense he'd seen during his recent Italian lunch, which made him appreciate the current place that much more, and unlike the damned fancy restaurant, they didn't have multiple forks and spoons.

This place seems okay. Wonder why it's going to have an asshole like Fifty-six here?

People in casual outfits filled most of the tables in the room and the stools around the bar, eating wings and potato skins and drinking beer while they waited for tonight's act to appear on the tiny wooden stage near the back of the room. A lonely microphone stand occupied the stage.

A few customers pointed James' way or took pictures with their cameras, but no one came over to harass him about selfies or autographs. He appreciated their restraint.

James swallowed his beer and grunted in satisfaction.

Even if Fifty-six's performance ended up being crap, the beer and wings were decent. If he lived closer to the place, he might stop by more often. The sauces might not be great, but they were definitely good.

Shay sat across from him, grinning.

"What's with the face?" James rumbled.

"It's just you." Shay shrugged. "I was thinking about how you were when I first met you, and how much you've changed."

"When you kept accusing me of being gay?"

Shay laughed. "Well, you've done a lot of good work in proving me wrong. No, it's just you wouldn't have even thought of something like this before."

James furrowed his brow. "Threatening a guy? I did that all the time before I met you. I did that shit a lot. Still do."

"No, thinking outside of the box." Shay shook her head. "You've always been a badass, but when I first met you, you weren't very flexible at anything that didn't involve creative ways of killing people, and now you have a business, friends, and a hot girlfriend. You know, an actual life." She winked.

James shrugged. "I do okay, and I *do* have a hot girlfriend, for sure."

A pale man in a khaki Nehru jacket marched onto the stage from a door in the back, a crystal wand in hand. A beige beret sat on top of his shaven head.

James grunted. "I think our guy is here, or at least his cousin."

Shay turned to him and snickered. "Yeah. That outfit does kind of scream pretentious douchebag."

The beige beret bearer approached the microphone and

tapped it with his wand. The dull roar of table and bar crosstalk died as everyone looked his way.

The wizard pointed his wand in the air. "I am Fifty-six." The number appeared in blue light above him. "I call myself that because I'm the fifty-sixth iteration of true musical paradigm advancement." He cut through the air with the wand, a line of ghostly blue musical notes following it. "Before the true return of magic we couldn't know true music, but now that it has returned, we can reach out to it in all its glory. Don't let the simple melodies of the Light Elves confuse you. That's not the true glory of magic." He gestured dramatically with his free hand. "We don't have to be stuck in backward paradigms that limit us to what is alleged to be acceptable. Melody. Rhythm. Chord progression. All primitive limits that can be denied with magic. As I control reality, I will exceed it."

Shay rolled her eyes. "I guess it's better he's doing this with magic than running around trying to kill people or something, but that'd probably be less painful than having to listen to this. I'm also pretty sure Forsythe could have hired a neighborhood guy to kick this guy's ass. Peyton could beat him up."

James chuckled.

Fifty-six stepped away from the microphone. "Grant me your attention now, my audience!" he shouted. "What you are about to hear will change everything you think you know about music."

"I wish I could forget about this guy already," Shay murmured.

The wizard flicked his wrist and arm back and forth as if his wand were a conductor's baton. Blue and red orbs of light winked into existence and disappeared with each movement. After a few seconds, they popped in and out of sight without any discernable link to Fifty-six's movements.

A harsh dissonant buzzing filled the air, several people shouting in surprise. The pitch of the buzz changed every few seconds without intelligible direction, and again with no connection to either the wizard's movement or the lights.

Crackling pops joined the buzzing. The wizard's movements sped up and he muttered something under his breath, most likely an incantation. A disconcerting warbling joined the wretched sonic tapestry passing for a performance.

James gritted his teeth, the obnoxious noises and total lack of anything approaching rhythm challenging his patience. Additional orbs of light of various colors kept appearing and reappearing at random spots on the stage, their materialization accompanied by buzzes, pops, or warbling.

Shay snickered, her face covered with amusement.

James rubbed his temples. "Is this modern music shit? Because this is some of the worst fucking crap I've ever heard. I think I'd rather go deaf than deal with this shit for more than a few minutes."

Shay leaned toward James and shook her head. "I think this is how the CIA breaks their interrogation subjects."

Given the loud boos and hisses coming from the crowd, apparently everyone shared James' and Shay's opinion about Fifty-six's performance.

The performance dragged on, despite the crowd

growing louder and unrulier, until a man in a vest and red nametag rushed onto the stage and waved his hands in front of Fifty-six's face.

"Please, just stop," the man, likely the manager, shouted. "I'll pay you twice as much if you stop."

The wizard lowered his wand and narrowed his eyes. The horrible soundscape ended, and cheers erupted from all around.

Fifty-six stomped toward the microphone with a sneer. "You are fools who don't understand the genius of what I just presented, but I don't care. Genius is always subjected to derision by the simple-minded, and the more you bourgeois lackwits challenge my True Music, the closer I move toward true artistic glory. In ten years, all music will be True Music."

"Someone call AET," a man in the back shouted. "I think that wizard just subjected me to magical torture."

Laughter rang through the club, including from Shay. James smiled. She was having a good time after all.

The wizard harrumphed and stormed off the stage and into the back room.

The manager walked over to the microphone. "I'm very, very sorry about that, folks. I don't know how that guy had the recommendations he did. Don't worry, everyone will get a free beer by way of apology."

Appreciative murmurs spread throughout the room.

Shay shook her head. "Well, we learned very few things, other than that guy is the musical equivalent of the plague."

James grunted. "I thought Anna was just being prissy when she talked about not wanting to be his muse, but damn, that shit was obnoxious."

"Sure." Shay picked up her half-empty beer to take a sip. "But he should be easy to freak out. Note that he didn't threaten the crowd with magic after their loud disagreement concerning the quality of his performance."

James picked up a wing. "Let's give him a few minutes." He nodded toward another door closer to the front. "Seen a lot of the staff come out of that door, so he might too."

Shay shrugged. "There could be a back door."

"You're right. Fuck it." James stood and set the wing down. "Let's just go."

Shay shook her head. "I'm staying out of it, remember?" She held up her beer. "Besides, I haven't finished my drink."

James grunted and marched toward the stage. "This won't take long."

The manager rushed toward him. "Sir, I understand that it was a terrible performance, but I'm going to have to ask you…" He blinked. "You're James Brownstone, aren't you? I didn't notice you before."

"Yeah, and I've got to have a talk with Fifty-six," James rumbled. "It doesn't have to do with that shit he calls music. Something else."

The manager ran his hands through his hair. "I didn't realize he had a bounty on him, I swear."

James opened his mouth to correct the man, then shrugged. A misunderstanding that got him easy access to the back was fine. This would be a quick conversation.

"Not your problem. It's *his* problem."

The manager nodded toward the door and rubbed his knuckles, a pained look on his face. "Our insurance isn't the best for this building."

James waved a hand. "Don't worry. I pay honest business owners if shit gets messed up."

The manager let out a sigh of relief.

James headed toward the stage door and threw it open. It led to a narrow hallway with a couple of doors. The hallway ended at an opening to a wide room and a door with a red glowing EXIT sign over it.

As the stage door closed behind him, James heard the manager on the microphone. "That's right, folks. We've got the Scourge of Harriken here going after a dangerous wizard bounty. Please stay in your seats until this matter is resolved."

The crowd cheered, and James snorted. The only thing Fifty-six was dangerous to was people's dignity.

James continued down the hallway until he reached the back room. The angry wizard paced back and forth between a few chairs, his back to the hallway and a long cigarette dangling from his mouth.

"Can't smoke in bars and clubs," James offered.

Fifty-six spun around. "Rules are for the common people, not glorious trendsetters." He narrowed his eyes at James. "I recognize you, but I can't place your face."

"Rules might be for common people, but stalking laws apply even to shitty musicians." James glared at the wizard.

Fifty-six dropped his cigarette to the tile floor and stubbed it out with his boot tip. He grabbed his wand from a nearby chair. "What are you talking about? What stalking?"

"Anna Forsythe. She says you're stalking her."

The wizard snorted. "Impossible, by definition. Are you a cop?"

James shook his head. "Consider me a concerned friend."

"Then you know what she is." The corner of Fifty-six's mouth turned up. "She's not human. Her existence is predicated upon being a muse to artists, but she's wasting it on crude and base blather. Do you know who she inspires right now? A stand-up comedian!" He shuddered. "Can you even wrap your mind around that? She's wasting her abilities to inspire some schlocky joke man." He slapped a hand on his chest hard. "While I am pushing the very boundaries of what music can be, and she refuses to become my muse! I even offered most of my life to her. She can't deny what is my right. She's not using her talent properly, so I've attempted to educate her. I haven't stalked her or anything so vulgar. A foolish woman needs persistence to understand intent, and as a genius, I'm allowed a certain latitude from traditional cultural mores."

James sighed and scratched his cheek. "Here's the thing, asshole. No, you fucking aren't. You're gonna leave Anna Forsythe alone, or we're going to have a very loud and painful one-way conversation."

Fifty-six tapped the wand on his cheek. "Oh, you poor, deluded thug. You're obviously not an artist, so I know she hasn't wasted her talents on you. She fluttered her eyelashes and promised you something?" He snorted. "She'll never give herself to a Neanderthal like you, and before you dare try to lay a hand on me, let that tiny little brain of yours reflect on the fact that I'm a wizard." He sneered. "Just because you didn't see harmful magic on stage doesn't mean I don't have it."

"You really don't know who I am, do you?" James shook

his head. "Now you're the poor deluded dumbass. I'm James Brownstone, asshole."

The wizard jumped back and raised his wand, his eyes narrowed. "You can't touch me, Brownstone. I'm not a criminal. I don't have a bounty on me."

James shrugged. "Don't give a fuck. I'm just giving you a warning. Anna doesn't want you sniffing around her anymore."

Fifty-six's face contorted in rage. "How dare you, you impudent classless clod! She's my destined muse, and she will inspire me to defeat the limitations and enter a realm of pure musical transcendence. I won't let anyone stop me."

Shit. Do I need to bond Whispy to deal with this asshole? Nah.

The wizard thrust his wand forward, and the air wavered in front of him. A loud screech assaulted James' ears, and he grunted and fell to one knee.

Fifty-six stepped toward James, his wand still pointed. "Too bad I've shattered your eardrums and you can't hear me now. You must be in agony, you stupid cretin. I should pop your head like a melon."

Heavy footfalls sounded from behind James. Shay barreled down the hallway, one of her knives out.

James stood and stuck out his palm to tell her to stop. "It's okay. I've got this." He turned back toward the wizard. "You're really starting to piss me off. You mentioned having no bounty? Fuck you. You've committed enough crimes against music to be punished, and you know what? I was gonna just give you a warning, but you just admitted you tried to rupture my eardrums, so now it's ass-kicking time."

Fifty-six gritted his teeth and pointed his wand again. James surged forward and slammed a fist into his face. The wizard flew backward and smashed partially through a wall with a groan, his nose broken and blood running down his face. His wand fell to the floor and rolled away.

James advanced toward the wizard and yanked him out of the wall. He tossed Fifty-six to the floor.

"Here's how this is going to go, asshole," he growled. "If I ever so much as hear you have mentioned Anna Forsythe's name, I'm gonna find you and bend you into a fucking pretzel." He knelt by the groaning wizard. "I fucking destroyed the Harriken, fought off the Council, and beat the Drow queen. You shouldn't have picked a fight you couldn't win. Do I make myself clear?"

"I...understand." Fifty-six moaned. "I'm...sorry."

James sighed. "Damn it." He pointed to the dent in the wall. "How much do you think it'll cost to fix that wall?"

CHAPTER NINE

The anti-sonic defense mode of Weber's tactical helmet had the pleasant secondary effect of damping the noise from the helicopter's rotors down to an easy-to-dismiss background thump rather than an all-encompassing cacophony. Combined with his in-helmet radio, he could speak to the team without having to yell.

Maria liked to yell; it was part of her leadership style. He preferred a stern but even-voiced approach.

"We're touching down in ten minutes," Weber explained to the team. "Dispatch got a report of a gang fight in progress at a junkyard in Wilmington, but we've got some sort of interference messing up transmissions and commands to any drones that get close and cameras in the area. We've got one eyewitness report that it's the Silver Ghost. Our team will hit that site, while the backup team is at the station on standby in case the Ghost rabbits."

"Interference?" Tracey replied. "Guess that explains why we haven't been able to get video or images of her."

McMahon turned his head toward Weber, although with his black helmet on, there was no way to read his expression. The black helmet with red AR goggles had been explicitly designed to make individual AET officers faceless and thus more intimidating. Sometimes they could win a surrender through sheer intimidation.

"We might have to put her down hard, you know," McMahon explained. "She might not give up just because a bunch of cops tell her to. I don't care if she's Oriceran or human—by the time you get to the point where you're dancing around the back alleys of LA killing people, you're past the point of chatting."

"We don't know that," Weber replied. "The FBI sent along some profile information. Although they are still adjusting their techniques to apply to Oricerans, and we don't know the Ghost's species for certain, in most cases, we can figure the psychology is somewhat similar when they are humanoid. On some level, the Silver Ghost wants the police to support her efforts. She likely believes she's helping us by cleaning up the city. If she's not Oriceran—if she's just a human with an artifact—that's even truer, but if we need to take her down, we'll do it. Safety first, ladies and gentlemen."

The officers all nodded.

Weber took a deep breath. "Everyone double-check your weapons and anti-magic deflectors. Preload anti-magic bullets. Given what we can tell from the 25K attack, we have no reason to believe conventional rounds will be effective. They did find anti-magic shell casings on site, but we're not sure when they started using them. They weren't able to recover any viable video from inside the restaurant

—probably because of the Ghost's apparent jamming abilities."

The eight AET officers on the helicopter all lifted and examined the crystals around their necks before they ejected their magazines from their rifles and put in new ones, except for the two officers with stun rifles.

Maybe we'll get lucky, and it'll turn out she's vulnerable to stun bolts. Don't want to have to hear the captain and the chief bitch about the budget if we use a bunch of anti-magic bullets.

Weber took a few more deep breaths. During his time in AET, he'd faced everything from demons to powerless men in costumes who had been mistaken for enhanced threats. Before each sortie, his stomach still tightened and his throat went dry.

Every cop who put on a uniform in the morning never knew if they were going to come home, and for AET, who had to throw themselves against the most dangerous threats the city had to offer, the risks were even worse.

Mark Johnson had died when the AET took on the Council, and even if Brownstone and his people had taken down the bastards, that death hung over every subsequent police operation. Armor and anti-magic deflectors might help protect an officer, but they couldn't guarantee he'd be able to drive home at the end of the day, especially when he could never be sure of the exact threat he might face.

"Remember our rules of engagement," Weber ordered. "I'll attempt to talk her down and get her to surrender, but if she attacks, we are to put her down hard. I don't care if she thinks she's cleaning up the city. She's breaking the law, and we're the law."

The armored AET officers jumped out of the helicopter on the outskirts of the junkyard, Weber in the lead. Landing too close to the battle site risked damage to the vehicle.

They rushed toward the screams and gunfire, their heavy footsteps thudding and echoing in the night to mingle with the sounds. Their AR goggles switched to night-vision mode and the eerie green, combined with the sounds of men dying, set a chilling atmosphere.

She'll surrender. She's a wannabe protector of the city. She probably looks up to AET. We'll end this without firing a single shot.

The AET rushed down the darkened dirt paths through the stacks of rusted-out cars and trucks until they arrived at a ramshackle workshop with rusted metal siding and a single open garage door, a few cars in various state of repair inside. Two late-model red Chevy SUVs were parked near the building, gleaming under the bright security lights surrounding the workshop.

Bodies and body parts lay all over the ground, along with guns. All were gang members, judging by their clothing and brightly colored bandanas. No one stirred, and Weber doubted any were alive, given the extent of their injuries.

Weber grimaced and threw up his hand to indicate the team should hold their positions. He tapped the side of his helmet to switch from night-vision mode to normal mode.

The AET officers stopped and formed a wedge, their weapons at the ready. They swept the area looking for an active target, but they only found more carnage.

Another scream sounded, and a man flew from behind the workshop. He landed in front of the officers, a burn several inches deep on his chest.

"Just like the bodies at the Kowloon," Weber muttered. "She's definitely here."

Weber let out a grim chuckle. That was LA. You could never be sure if a massacre was because of any particular enhanced psycho. Brownstone was helping cut down on that problem, but he was only one man, in the end. The cops were still the main wall keeping the barbarians in check.

A few seconds later, a blur of movement caught Weber's attention, and the silver-skinned vigilante landed in the middle of the bodies, one of her arms in a bladed form.

Weber blinked, marveling at the lithe form for a moment. She matched the few rumors and witness descriptions the police had managed to cobble together, but seeing the faceless silver-skinned woman in front of him drove her reality into his brain in a way even the Kowloon massacre hadn't.

"This is the LAPD AET," Weber announced. "You are to immediately drop any weapons, deactivate any artifacts, and surrender. You're under arrest for murder and destruction of property. Any sudden movements will be considered hostile actions, and you will be fired upon."

The Silver Ghost didn't move for several seconds, and Weber let out a sigh of relief. If she was thinking about what he'd just ordered, she had to realize she was outgunned, and if they were right and she respected police like Brownstone did, this would all be over in seconds.

"No," the Silver Ghost replied, her words unnerving

because the clear voice came from her otherwise feature-less face. "I will not surrender. My testing and calibration aren't done yet. I will give you, the guardians of order in this city, one chance to flee. If not, I can't guarantee your safety."

The AET officers on the flanks began spreading out, keeping their weapons at the ready.

Weber gritted his teeth. So much for a quick surrender.

"Put your hands on your head and deactivate your artifacts," he shouted, moving his finger toward the trigger. "We've got armor, anti-magic bullets, and anti-magic deflectors; you can't win. I know you think you're doing us a favor, but you've violated the law. If you surrender right now, I'm sure we can arrange leniency for your cooperation."

Come on. You're supposed to be on our side. Just give the hell up.

The Silver Ghost's head turned back and forth as if she were surveying the eight officers in front of her. "This is an excellent opportunity. All my testing and calibration has been against foes of limited capabilities. Even the ones using magic have been a disappointment, and most have been cowards, like all parasites."

"Stun her," Weber ordered.

The harsh buzz of the two stun rifles firing filled the air. The blue stun bolts flew toward the Ghost and struck her, arcing over her body like ghostly fingers. She didn't collapse, move, or even twitch.

The officers fired again, but the silver-skinned woman didn't go down. At least if she'd had a face, they might be able to tell if she was in pain.

The Silver Ghost raised her non-bladed arm. "If you don't fight in earnest, you'll die." A golden energy blast shot from her arm and struck one of the officers with a stun rifle. He screamed and fell back.

"Take her down!" Weber shouted.

The AET officers opened up with a volley so tight and synchronized that someone might think they practiced daily. Six anti-magic bullets and one stun bolt would be enough to take down the vast majority of criminals, human or Oriceran. The bullets struck the Ghost's body, some making shallow, dark indentations, and a few blasting clean through her, leaving gaping holes, but there was no sign of blood or internal organs. It was like she was nothing but silver metal.

I don't know what species she is. Maybe she's related to some of those rock guys they briefed us about last week?

Weber spared a glance at the downed officer and frowned. His anti-magic deflector was still clear, not even a speck of darkness.

What the hell? That was obviously an energy attack. It had to be magic.

They kept up their fire, but the Silver Ghost's wounds, if they could even be called that, started to seal. She rushed toward the AET's right flank and sliced with her blade, cutting clean through the armor and into the chest of McMahon. He groaned and collapsed, blood seeping out onto this armor.

Weber switched to the burst fire and concentrated his attacks on the Ghost's head. She jerked a few times, backing away.

"McMahon? Tracey?" Weber shouted. "You still with us?"

Both responded only with groans, but at least they responded.

Weber's rifle clicked empty, and he ejected the magazine as the other officers kept up single shots. He slapped in a new magazine, his heart racing.

Why the hell aren't the anti-magics taking her down? Shit, is there a counterspell to anti-magic bullets?

The Silver Ghost sprinted forward and leapt into the air, bringing her foot up at the same time. Her kick landed hard against a man's chest and sent him flying ten feet back into a rusted-out Buick Skylark with a crunch.

Before she even landed, she swung her blade and cut through the armor and into the shoulder of another man. She pulled the blade back and kicked the wounded officer in the back. He groaned in pain and hit the ground, rolling several times before coming to a stop.

Another point-blank energy blast downed another cop, a hole burned clean through his armor into his leg. He screamed.

Damn it, have to think of alternatives. No defense is perfect.

Weber took a few steps back and ceased fire, then yanked a sonic grenade off his tactical belt. He primed and threw it, confident his team's helmets would protect them.

The grenade went off with its tell-tale high-pitched whine right above the Silver Ghost, but the vigilante didn't stop her latest attack as she sliced through a rifle and slammed her elbow into a man with enough force to send him flying backward several yards.

The lieutenant wasn't sure how long it'd been since they'd initiated the engagement. Less than a minute, probably. Perhaps even less than thirty seconds, but the rest of his team lay on the ground wounded, maybe even dead, and their enemy hadn't so much as slowed down.

His breathing ragged, Weber tried to figure out his options. Bullets didn't work. Stun rifles didn't work. Sonic grenades didn't work. He tossed his rifle to the ground and pulled out his combat knife. It might be a desperate sliver of hope, but he'd take what he could get.

The Silver Ghost stalked toward him. "You would still stand and fight after that?"

"You cop-killing bitch," Weber shouted through gritted teeth. "There's no way I'm letting you get away with that. You're going down."

"Don't worry, none of your people are dead. I decided to also use this calibration session as a chance to test modulation. It helps with stability." The Silver Ghost's head turned toward one of the downed men. "Well, they aren't dead yet, and I'm sure ambulances and medical helicopters will come quickly for police officers."

Weber bellowed a challenge and charged with the knife. She met his advance with a powerful kick to the chest. The blow crumpled both his armor and his ribs. He groaned as pain radiated from his chest. The jolting impact of hitting the ground summoned more.

The Silver Ghost walked up to him and lowered her blade until it hovered a few inches above his head. "Bravery in the face of insurmountable odds is commendable but ultimately pointless. It's an epiphany I had when I was forced to take extreme measures. Brave men and women might stand against a monster, but if they die, what have they accomplished? Sometimes discretion really is the better part of valor."

Weber grimaced. He reached up and pulled off his helmet, desperate for some fresh air. "You've made a big mistake." Taking quick, shallow breaths only did so much to dull the pain in his chest. "You just attacked...the LAPD. Now you're...an...attempted cop killer." His gaze wavered, and he looked down at his still-clear magic deflector.

Why didn't they work?

"No," the Silver Ghost replied. "It was you who made the mistake. I didn't kill you outright only because I understand that sometimes a person has to follow orders, but you had no reason to engage me when I was confining myself to monsters and parasites. I'm above you. Better than you, but that's a good thing, because I can protect you from the true monsters. Don't you police already admit that by allowing bounty-hunting scum to wander LA?"

Distant sirens sounded, and the Silver Ghost's blade arm reverted to a normal arm, hand, and fingers.

"This isn't...Oriceran," Weber pushed out. "What about our...rules and laws?"

The Silver Ghost let out a dark chuckle. "Without force, rules and laws are meaningless. A fiction. I've witnessed that my entire life. Why don't you ask one of your precious bounty hunters for help? Make it a good one. I need further calibration and testing." She gave a little wave and burst into a sprint, her form quickly disappearing into the night.

Weber stared at the sky and managed a smile despite his pain.

That's right, bitch. Bounty hunters like Brownstone. You're going down.

CHAPTER TEN

James bolted upright, the room pitch-black except for one small light source on his nightstand: his ringing phone. He frowned and jerked his head toward the cause of his quick awakening.

He never shut his phone off on the off-chance Alison might call him for help in the middle of the night. He didn't care if she was at a magic school surrounded by wizards and witches. The faint worry that something dangerous was always lingering around her never left his head, and he was ready to hop on a plane and kill whatever threatened his daughter.

Shay rolled onto her side. "Answer or ignore the call already. I'm trying to sleep here, and you exhausted me earlier. Plus, I was having the most wonderful dream about Alan crying and agreeing to do a haka if I would stay at the university." She chuckled wearily.

James grabbed the phone and looked at the caller ID.

Maria Hall.

He frowned. Maria wouldn't call him in the middle of the night without a damned good reason.

"What's up, Maria?" James answered.

She took a deep breath before replying. "Have you heard of the Silver Ghost?"

James frowned. "Yeah, but I haven't been paying much attention. Rumors about some Oriceran vigilante chick who has messed with a few gangs in the last month or two. I've been taking it easy, so I haven't looked into it. Plus, as far as I've heard she doesn't have a bounty, so she's not really my business."

"Not just rumors," Maria replied. "She's real and powerful. She can survive high-powered rifle shots, stun rifles, and shotguns, and is resistant to at least some bladed weapons. Massive regeneration. Wounds healing just seconds after she's taken them. She's fast, can jump onto at least one-story buildings with ease, and she's strong. Probably as strong as you, if not stronger. She also can fire energy blasts that are lethal with one shot and tunnel right through high-quality tactical armor. To be honest, other than you, she might be one of the most tactically-threatening enhanced individuals in the city. There was no wand or incantations involved."

"Okay, that's all interesting, I guess, but why the fuck should I care? Why are you calling me in the middle of the night to tell me about her? It's not my business if she's killing gang members. That's cop shit to solve."

Shay groaned. "So tired…"

Maria sighed. "The thing is, I just got a call from my old captain. He explained to me that the department's been tracking her activities for a while, but was trying to keep a lid on things to prevent a lot of magical types or humans with artifacts from playing nighttime vigilante with no regulation or oversight and turning the entire city into a war zone."

James nodded. "That explains why I hadn't heard much when I didn't go looking. But there's more to this? The gangs taking out big hits on her, maybe? Bringing in outside magical types as muscle?"

"You didn't hear on the news about the Kowloon massacre?" Maria sounded surprised.

"Nah. Haven't been paying much attention to non-barbeque-related news. Trying to take it easy lately. That's part of taking it easy, and I don't give much of a shit about the news anyway."

"The Silver Ghost killed pretty much everyone in the local 25K Triad the other night," Maria explained. "Quickly and brutally. The police have been trying to stall with talk of violence between organized crime groups, but the rumors are spreading far and wide that the Silver Ghost was involved."

James grunted. "Still don't see what this has to do with me."

Maria groaned. "Look, here's the problem. Yesterday, an AET team led by Weber sortied to capture the Silver Ghost. The higher-ups want her contained. When she was picking off a criminal here and there, I think they weren't worried, but now she's cleaning out entire gangs. No one knows who or what she is, which means the police can't begin to get a handle on her. The PDA is starting to get involved, but they're having trouble as well because the cops don't have any items or tissue samples to help them with their tracking magic."

James frowned. "Did something happen with the AET when they took on the Silver Ghost?"

"She took them down *hard*. The AET budget for healing potions is limited. Half the team are still in the hospital. Several have been discharged after treatment, but they will be out of action for weeks, if not months. Weber is in surgery. Multiple broken ribs, and by the time the paramedics got there, he had a collapsed lung, too. They say he'll make it, but the poor bastard just got promoted, and now will be benched for a while."

James grunted. "What the fuck? So this Silver Ghost, who is supposed to be a vigilante targeting criminals, nearly killed a bunch of cops?"

Shay sat up with a frown.

"That's the summary version, yes." Maria took a deep breath. "It gets worse. Much worse."

"How could it get worse?"

"The team went in very well prepared," Maria explained. "They already knew her general capabilities because of the Kowloon massacre, so they showed up with anti-magic deflectors and anti-magic bullets loaded. Here's the weird part: the anti-magic deflectors didn't work. Every cop they could get a statement from confirmed that, and they showed no signs of having absorbed any magic."

"The anti-magic deflectors didn't work?" James frowned deeply. "I didn't know that was possible."

"It's fucking magic, so anything's possible. Maybe. I don't know. The point is, they didn't work, and cops got hurt."

Shay grabbed her phone and started tapping.

James thought over the possibilities for a few seconds. "Maybe it was just because she was only using certain types of attacks."

"Part of it was because she turned her arm into a kind of sword, and I get that," Maria replied. "It's just force, and apparently she's strong enough and has a sharp enough sword to cut through AET tactical armor, but she also fired those energy blasts; gold, from the description. Not like anything I've heard of in terms of conventional weapons, and the blasts went right through AET armor with the anti-magic deflectors not doing anything. No change in color, nothing. They might as well have not even been wearing them."

James rubbed his chin. "Maybe it's some sort of advanced government prototype weapon from the CIA or Russia or China or something? If some terrorist got their hands on it, maybe they're testing it, or maybe they're even deliberately using American criminals to test it."

Maria snorted. "You don't pay much attention to cutting-edge weapons tech, do you, Brownstone?"

Shay continued typing on her phone, her brow furrowed.

"Nope. Don't need it," James replied. "My tools work for me. Why would I want complicated gadgets that can just break down?"

Maria chuckled darkly. "Here's the thing: the best tech in the field is stuff like the exoskeletons you see Special Forces use, along with railguns and that kind of weapon. If you're talking actual vehicles, the military's got some fancy energy shit, but as far as personal weapons, no. Even on the horizon, they're talking powered armor that will probably hit general field use for the military in five years and may filter down to the units like AET in ten years. That powered armor is mostly just about carrying more stuff around; greater mobility, better armor, and bigger guns." She sucked in a deep breath. "The Silver Ghost isn't in power armor, though. We don't have any pictures of her because somehow she's jamming recording devices, but basically, the witnesses all say the same thing. She looks like an athletic naked chick who just happens to have silver skin, but she has no face, and her energy blasts come out of her arm, not a weapon. That isn't a Russian or Chinese experimental weapon. Her skin can't be tech because no one has technology like that, which means it's magical, except somehow she's immune to anti-magic bullets. In other words, our worst-case scenario: an Oriceran who we don't have a real hard counter for."

James grunted. "This shit is obnoxious."

"That's one way to describe it. I'm calling you for two reasons. First of all, the city and county of Los Angeles are putting out an official level-five bounty on the Silver Ghost. Second, I want to ask you as a personal favor to go after her. The captain called me specifically to convince you to get involved. I'd love to grab some of the guys and do it myself, but she just laid out a fully-equipped AET team. Even if we had Trey and his gloves, we'd get our asses handed to us. There's probably only one man in LA who can handle the Silver Ghost. Fight fire with fire, and fight a Silver Ghost with a Granite Ghost."

James snorted. "Okay, fair enough. One question: is the bounty dead or alive?"

"Yeah, it is," Maria murmured. "And personally, I'd strongly prefer dead. This woman's out of control. If she's at the point now where she's taking down cops, it won't be long before she starts attacking anyone and everyone who offends her sensibilities. Maybe I don't have the best track record when it comes to pointing out people who might be dangerous, but this woman isn't like you, Brownstone. She's not even trying to obey the law, and it's obvious from the attacks and what she told the AET officers she took down that she doesn't respect the police. This will escalate unless you stop her. It's going to end with dead civilians and dead cops."

Shay stared at her phone for a moment. "Son of a bitch." *What is she even doing?*

"Do you have any leads other than what she looks like?"

"Yeah, one weird thing about this is that we've got sightings in both Los Angeles and Las Vegas, although most of her action has been in Los Angeles."

"Los Angeles and Las Vegas?" James echoed. He frowned. "Fine, I'll find her and take her down. I don't care how badass she thinks she is, she hasn't fought *me* yet."

"Exactly." Maria let out a sigh of relief. "Thanks, Brownstone. Just hurry up. Next time, she might actually finish the cops off." She ended the call.

James tossed his phone on the nightstand. "I wonder if this shit is my fault?"

Shay looked up from her phone. "If I understood what I was overhearing, and I hope I did because I woke Peyton up by texting to get him moving, it sounds like this Silver Ghost vigilante hurt cops?"

"Yeah, but Maria says she operates mostly in Los

Angeles and Las Vegas." James frowned. "The name, too: Silver Ghost. It's too damned close to Granite Ghost."

"What about it?" Shay snorted at a text on her phone and rolled her eyes. "Stop whining, Peyton. We're all awake now."

James shook his head. "When my rep started getting bigger, I thought it was a good thing. It'd keep the shitbags in check, but what if this woman took the wrong lesson? If she's trying to be me, it might have led to those cops getting hurt."

"Dial down the Catholic guilt for a second, James." Shay snorted. "You being at fault is bullshit. You might very well be the toughest badass on this planet at this point, at least when you get pissed. You soloed the Drow queen and won, let alone all the other shit and people you've taken down, but you've never gone after cops, even when you're all full of hate and anger and Whispy's egging you on." She held up her phone. "Peyton gave me the quick executive summary of what she's been involved in, and it's obvious she's a nutjob. The thing is, she's a nutjob who is either a powerful Oriceran or a human who got herself a nice little artifact. What's her deal? What can she do?"

James related what Maria had told him.

"Huh." Shay pursed her lips. "That regeneration's nasty, but I'm willing to bet if you got in there and did your thing, it wouldn't last long. Whispy probably just needs a few good hits before he can adapt and figure out something. Plus, she's obviously not invulnerable, because otherwise, she wouldn't be worrying so much about hiding. The best thing to do is track her down and beat her down."

James grunted. "I plan to. Just have to find her first.

Because of that jamming ability, it's gonna get annoying." James let out a low growl. "Which means it won't just be a matter of flooding the city with drones and letting Heather and Peyton do their thing. Once we find her, though, I don't think I'll have much trouble getting into advanced mode." He curled his hands into fists. "You're right, Shay. Who knows who this bitch is, but it doesn't matter. The only thing that matters is stopping her."

CHAPTER ELEVEN

Unlike Shay, James waited until morning to call Heather. He laid out the situation in a succinct manner as he fried some eggs. Shay remained in bed, which was fine with him. She'd already sicced Peyton on the target, and now this was his problem to solve, not hers.

The thought that he'd somehow inspired the Silver Ghost lingered, even if he no longer brooded about the possibility. If a man created a problem, the simplest solution was to solve the problem himself, and that was what he intended to do. Now that he was armed with a plan, the only direction left was forward. He didn't doubt for a second that he could track the Ghost down, even if the police were having trouble.

Things aren't like in the old days. I have an entire fucking team I can use to take the Ghost down. She might have a few tricks, but I've got a lot of good people. We can find her and win this. I don't give a shit if she regenerates. So do I.

"I've seen a little bit about her on the dark web," Heather explained, "but until the Kowloon massacre, most people thought she was just an urban legend or some sort of FBI psy-ops construct, or even an Oriceran psychology experiment. I wasn't taking her seriously, and it didn't seem like something that would involve you, so I paid even less attention. I kind of regret that now."

"No reason to worry about the past. Let's just think about what we're going to do going forward." James grunted and started plating his eggs. "And she's real enough to kill a lot of people and hurt cops. What I don't get is that it seems like she came out of nowhere. Or am I wrong about that?"

"I'll have to check more, but from what little I've been seeing, no. No sightings before six weeks ago. There have been other reports of powerful silver-skinned women both before and after the gates opened, but none of them match her description in terms of powers, and most don't have the whole weird missing-face thing. Whoever or whatever she is, she only set up shop recently."

He set his plate on the table and took a seat, downing a quick bite of eggs while he nestled the phone between his shoulder and neck. Eggs were okay, even if they weren't ribs.

"That means she's probably more likely to be a human who stumbled on an artifact than an Oriceran," James rumbled. "That'd explain why she came out of nowhere. I've seen this kind of shit a lot with bounties. Some loser gets their hands on an artifact, and the next week they're giving themselves an alias and going to town."

Heather chuckled. "Just to be clear...from what I can tell, other people gave her that name. She didn't do it herself."

"Same thing. Probably a crime victim. Maybe she's a rich woman who paid a tomb raider to bring her artifacts so she could start her own war on crime. Peyton might be able to find out something working that angle."

"Maybe." The clack of Heather's keyboard came over the line for a few moments. "One thing that sticks out to me already are a few references from witnesses who overheard her. They say she's mentioned 'calibration and testing.'"

James swallowed another bite of eggs before responding, "Yeah, Maria sent me a copy of the police report. The cops, even the chief, all want me to solve this for them. The hurt AET guys also mentioned something about calibration and testing." He frowned. "Now that I think about it, maybe I'm wrong about this being an artifact."

"How do you figure?"

"Maybe I'm wrong and Maria's wrong, and this is some experimental foreign weapon. Calibration and testing sounds like something you do with a weapon, not spells, doesn't it?"

Heather sighed. "Don't know since I'm not a witch, but they have to test that stuff out, too. Even if it's not pure magic, technomagic is a known thing. There are a few start-ups looking into that. Maybe this is technomagic. That might explain how they beat the anti-magic deflectors, but I'm far from an expert, so I can't be sure. Maybe we should bring in magical types to help."

James frowned. "We've got Victoria. I'd get Dannec involved, but if the PDA is having trouble, I doubt he can help, and I don't trust his ass like I trust you, Peyton, or my guys. I've got ways of beating magic as long as I get close to the Silver Ghost, so I'm not worried about that. We just need to find her."

"Understood. So, what's the general plan?"

"I can't take her down if I'm not near her, so the first thing we need to do is find her or at least figure out where she might end up. Is there anything you can do to find her? If she's blocking recordings and electronics and shit, you can't just run drones at her, right?" James frowned. "Or do you have some way around that?"

The most annoying aspect of dealing with increasingly dangerous enemies was how complicated things involving them got. In the old days, he'd run a man down in a day or two, maybe stop in to chat with an informant. Nowadays, when dealing with people like the Council, he was having to be careful and spend weeks tracking targets before confronting them.

I tried and tried and tried to keep my life simple, but it just didn't work. Wonder if I made things more complicated by trying to keep things simple?

Some days, James wondered if it'd just be easier to have Heather set up a website where he could issue public challenges and specify the time and date for the bounty to show up. Despite how angry Shay became over his pay-per-view, he won against Lars in the end. Though, upon reflection, he didn't have a good way of limiting a showdown to a specific bounty. If he tried something like that, it'd probably end up even worse than the ambush situation with Lars.

Would it be so bad if a bunch of guys showed up? If I went into extended advanced mode, I could clean up a whole group of bastards at once. I've got a lot more control and understanding of Whispy these days.

The simplest solution would probably be to take down multiple guys at once.

"James?" Heather prodded.

He grunted and blinked. He'd tuned her out while thinking about his Tyler-esque website scheme. "Sorry, got distracted. What did you say again?"

Heather sighed. "What I was saying is that I can't track her directly, but I can *potentially* track her."

"Huh? I don't understand how you can track if you can't track her. Is this some Zen riddle shit?"

Heather chuckled. "No, nothing like that. You just have to think about this situation in a different way. Sometimes you don't look for evidence; you look for an absence of evidence where there should be some. Just like if you were following footprints in the mud, and you suddenly don't see them. That tells you something happened, and you'd know to look around the area where the footprints disappeared even more thoroughly for clues."

"That makes sense," James replied, pleased that others on his team could handle complicated analysis without him having to lead them by the nose. "So you have ideas? Whatever she's using to mess up recordings might extend to the net, especially if it's magic. You're not even magic, and you were still able to remove those recordings of Shay from the net." He took another bite of his eggs and glanced at Thomas, who slumbered peacefully in the living room, his head resting on his paws. For a dog who wasn't that old, he sure liked to sleep a lot.

Probably live a long time because of it. Maybe I should sleep more.

"Admittedly, this is going to be harder than a normal job," Heather replied. "But there's no magic so thorough that it can erase all indirect traces of people, even with some of the new hotshot infomancer-type wizards who have been showing up lately. Even that shit I did with Shay… I might have deleted the videos, but a good hacker who looked into the situation would know something had been there and was now gone. Besides, we don't have to worry about that kind of thing."

James grunted. "Why don't we? I'm not a hacker, but it sounds like it's important."

"We already know she can't do that," Heather replied, her grin audible in her voice.

"We do? How do we know that?"

"Yes, we do. Think about it. The fact there are witness statements is proof she can't erase herself from everyone's memory, and some of these witness statements are on the net, which also suggests she's not actively going around removing every reference to herself. Since we have those trails, that means Peyton and I can find something if we just approach this the right way. Especially since she's limiting herself to Los Angeles and Vegas."

James chuckled. "Only Los Angeles and Las Vegas? That's a lot of people and ground to cover. They aren't exactly small cities."

Heather snorted dismissively. "Maybe, but they represent a tiny fraction of the world's landmass and population, so compared to some of the searches we've had to do in the past, it's pathetically simple to focus in on."

"Glad someone thinks so."

"Besides, the Silver Ghost might have a few tricks, but she hasn't faced two world-class hackers and the world's toughest bounty hunter before. It's only a matter of time now that we're targeting her. I don't care who she is and what artifacts or spells she might have access to, she's just one woman. There's been no information about her having friends, and not even any information to suggest she can teleport or portal, which means she's limited in her mobility."

"Good point." James grunted. "Concentrate more on Los Angeles. All her big moves have been here, not in Vegas, and the fact she took down the 25K Triad, that gang, and the AET recently in LA makes me think she's gearing up for more here."

"Okay, sounds like a plan. I'll coordinate directly with Peyton on this."

"Good. If you get any hits for Vegas, pass the information directly to Trey for follow-up. He's still in Vegas for a few days."

"I will," Heather replied. "Anything else for now?"

"Nope," James rumbled. "Need leads before we can figure out where to go from here. Talk to you later, but if you get anything, call or text me right away. I want to take this bitch down before she kills a cop."

"I'll do my best to find her." Heather ended the call.

James immediately dialed Trey. Hackers were a tool, and a useful one, but he'd had a long career without a dedicated hacker on his team. A man hitting the street and informants would always have a place in the bounty hunter's arsenal.

After James finished the explanation, Trey's response wasn't unexpected or out of line.

"Damn, big man. This Silver Ghost sounds like a crazy bitch. I've heard a little bit about her from people, but I wasn't sure she was real. I mean, you know what they say: seeing is believing. You're on tv and shit, and I haven't even seen a picture of her." Trey sucked in a breath. "That shit is crazy though, taking down the AET when she's supposed to be some sort of vigilante. I'm thinking she was just limiting herself to crooks because she thought the police wouldn't come after her if she did. Probably just a psycho who likes killing people."

"Yeah," James replied. "That might be the case. I want this shit high-priority. Top priority. Drop any other boun-ties you're working there. I don't give a shit how close you are to finding them, and I don't give a shit who it is or what they've done. I want every man in Vegas working the informants and finding any fucking tiny-ass scrap of infor-mation they can get their hands on that might possibly lead us to the Silver Ghost. Heather and Peyton are doing their thing, but they might not be able to find her the usual ways. We need to find the Silver Ghost so I can go put an end to her bullshit. I'll give a huge-ass bonus to anyone who gives me the tip that leads to her, and I'll be splitting the bounty among everyone working this job."

Trey whistled. "Rare to hear you so worked up. Don't worry, I'll let the boys and Victoria know. We'll track this silver bitch down and let you do your thing."

CHAPTER TWELVE

A couple of days later, James and Shay stepped out of her Fiat into Warehouse Two. The loading bay door closed behind them, the rumble of the motor echoing in the spacious warehouse.

Every time I come here, I can't help but notice all the wasted space. Shay probably could have gotten by with a couple of warehouses. How much of it is because she needed it, and how much of it is because she thought it was cool?

Shay headed toward the office, James trailing behind. He looked around, his gaze landing on the orange ball of fur hiding in the shadows. The cat stared at him, a far-too-hungry look in his eyes.

Fucking cat. Probably planning how to eat us when we die. You can't win while I'm still breathing, cat.

James grunted. He didn't trust cats. A dog was a loyal friend of humanity, but he half-suspected that if cats ever managed to get opposable thumbs, it'd be lights out for the human race. Oddly enough, feline humanoid races from Oriceran, at least the few he'd met, didn't bother him.

He didn't worry about the inconsistency and would admit to anyone who asked that his feelings toward cats could be the result of a bounty hunter's instinct or the simple bias of a dog owner.

No other hungry, traitorous pets waited in the warehouse as they closed on the office where Peyton sat at his computer.

They stepped inside. One of his monitors displayed Heather, a headset on, her hair a mess. She looked like she hadn't slept in days.

James hadn't done much better, spending most of his time on the streets. He'd been hitting informants of all types, but his efforts had yet to yield any useful new information. As the Granite Ghost, James was a fixture in Los Angeles, a known quantity with known haunts. The Silver Ghost was more elusive, a spectral presence who appeared for a kill and then disappeared.

"Okay," Shay began, moving to the far wall. "We need to go over everything we have so far. I know it's only been a couple of days since we started looking into things, but we've been lucky the Silver Ghost hasn't made another move. Given the scale of her last couple of attacks, the next assault will probably involve a huge number of people. I think we're at the point where people other than criminals will get killed. She's already hurt some cops."

James gritted his teeth.

Good thing Alison's in school right now where she's safe. I don't care who this Silver Ghost is. She won't be able to win against an entire school filled with witches and wizards.

He nodded. "I contacted Tyler and Kathy to have them look into things on their end. If the Ghost is targeting mostly criminals, that means the underworld should have the most chatter. Kathy's got her ear to the ground for anything useful, and Tyler's been trying to listen in about the Ghost since she first appeared, including hitting some of his scummiest underworld contacts. If anything, he's trying extra hard because I think he figures he'll be the new Eyes if he can score information on her that no one else has."

Shay snorted. "And did he find out anything useful?"

"Shit so far, or at least, nothing we don't already know about the Ghost." James shrugged. "No one knows anything about who the Silver Ghost actually is or where she's from. They all know her victim list, but there's no real pattern there. Street gangs, individual thugs and hitmen, and bigger organized groups like the 25K Triad. As far as Tyler knows, there's no link between the groups." He frowned. "The police are saying the same thing, so it's not like some woman who got killed in a drive-by and was raised by a necromancer or some shit."

"You're saying there's absolutely no link at all between the victims? Excluding the AET, of course."

James shook his head. "A few had dealings, but only minor, and most of them haven't had any at all. The only thing Tyler seemed certain of was that everyone's shitting a brick over her. They're afraid the Ghost might come after them. The cops are right to worry. Some of the bigger organizations are reaching out for muscle, particularly magical muscle. If they don't end up fighting the Silver Ghost, they'll probably end up fighting each other." He shifted his gaze from Peyton to Heather on the screen. "Maria passed along some more information, but the cops don't have much either. They've been too worried about what she called 'contagious vigilantism and escalation.' They're finally starting to move, but still pretty slowly. I think they want to see what I shake out of the trees before making too much noise."

Peyton nodded. "I've been able to confirm what the police are saying. There's definitely missing camera and drone footage whenever the Silver Ghost appears, but it's not perfect invisibility. I've found footage of her in long-range shots. Not exactly great for details, but I can at least confirm where she's appeared."

Shay smiled. "Good job, Peyton."

He shrugged. "Not that it does us much good. All it proves is that she can't fly. We already knew that, but at least there's no evidence of a helicopter or anything like that picking her up. She just does her thing and takes off, and at some point, the cameras and drones lose track of her."

Heather cleared her throat and leaned back in her chair, the strong backlighting in her room shadowing her face. "I've been trying to cross-reference everything to confirm the relative frequency of her appearances. Basically trying to make sure she's been hitting LA more than Vegas, and it seems to be true. About four to one in appearances, although all her big kills have been here. I don't know what to make of that pattern."

Shay frowned and shook her head. "I was afraid of that."

Everyone looked her way, but it was James who asked the obvious question. "What do you mean? Afraid of what?"

"It's been bothering me since the beginning." Shay

shook her head. "Why LA and Vegas? Why those two cities?"

"She's probably from or lives in one or the other." Peyton shrugged. "They're close to each other and connected by major highways."

"Which describes pretty much every major city in the United States, let alone California." Shay shook her head. "If it's just about convenience or distance, why not, say, San Diego? Why Vegas? San Diego's closer to the border, too, so she could hop over to Mexico and beat on people there. She doesn't seem to care about following the law, and she's not a bounty hunter who has to worry about license restrictions."

James chuckled. "Maybe she's stopping off at Jessie Rae's between kills."

Shay spun toward him, a serious expression on her face. "I think that's closer to the truth than you might want to believe."

Peyton laughed. "What? We don't even know if she eats, but we haven't found anything that suggests she likes barbeque."

Shay shook her head. "James said it himself—the possibility of her being inspired by him, and it's stuck in my head ever since. I just needed some time to let it work through. A woman who has external armor with a blade and an energy blast who is hanging out mostly in LA and Las Vegas and calls herself the Silver Ghost? It's too damned close to James and the Granite Ghost. Close enough that I do wonder if it's a coincidence."

Heather looked down at the monitor for a moment, perhaps checking something on her computer before looking up and shrugging. "So what? If she's inspired by James, that's helpful how? It's not like he has a particular hunting pattern we can follow."

James nodded. "Yeah, true enough."

Shay sighed. "If only it ended there. We have to think of the other big clue in all this."

James frowned. "Other big clue?"

"Yeah. Besides her obsessive focus on Las Vegas and Los Angeles and similar general types of attacks, there's one huge clue that's been bugging me, but everyone, including the cops, keeps coming to the wrong conclusion." Shay let out a grim chuckle. "Of course they do, because it's a matter of paradigm, and even though I knew better, I still found myself thinking about this the old-fashioned way."

What the fuck is she talking about? Am I the only one who is lost here?

Peyton frowned. "I'm really, really lost, Shay."

Huh. Guess not. Thanks, Peyton.

Shay crossed her arms and leaned against the wall. "The AET team got their ass handed to them because their anti-magic bullets didn't do anything special and their anti-magic deflectors didn't work."

"Yeah, so?" Peyton shrugged. "James doesn't have to depend on that kind of thing. If he finds her, he'll pound her."

"Don't you see? Anti-magic bullets are just normal bullets that pierce magical defenses." Shay shook her head. "If there's no magic involved, they aren't any better than normal bullets. But everyone keeps assuming that the Silver Ghost *has* to be magical because her attacks don't make sense otherwise. That's bullshit, though. It presumes we have only two choices: Earth technology or Oriceran magic. We all know there are third, fourth, and probably fifth, if not infinite, options."

James grunted, and Heather and Peyton grimaced simultaneously.

Shay nodded slowly. "Exactly. A powerful non-magical personal energy weapon that doesn't require a long barrel or a dish or something? Not something you see with Earth tech, but definitely achievable by an alien woman with access to programmable nanites. When James fought the nanoform, it used different sorts of energy attacks. A mysterious woman who is powerful is sniffing around the places James goes and has non-magical weapons that are well beyond Earth tech. It has to be the alien bitch. She's scoping out her prey's environment, pulling huntress shit."

"That might explain why she's so good at jamming drones and cameras." Peyton scratched his chin. "She must have learned her lesson from Heather and me going after her and isn't willing to risk anything more than local inter-ference. If we can't trace her, we can't find her."

Heather's eyes widened, and she nodded quickly. "Whatever she's doing isn't an EMP either, since normal function is restored after she leaves the area. The high level of jamming, considering she has no vehicle to carry around a jammer, would be difficult normally, but it makes sense if she has access to alien tech."

James frowned. "I don't get it, though. If it's the alien woman, why is she attacking random people? Why not come straight at me?"

Shay shook her head. "Not random people, violent criminals. I don't know what the hell happened to her in the past, and she obviously played me with the lance thing, but Erin spent a decade running a refugee charity. She obviously thinks of herself as some sort of champion of the downtrodden."

"But what about the cops? AET hunts dangerous criminals, too."

"That's the trick, though. She *didn't* go after AET." Shay shook her finger. "The AET went after *her*. I read the police report. They even admit in the report that she gave them a chance to run away, and even though she beat them down like a Kilomea MMA fighter taking on a pixie, she didn't go for the easy kills."

James snorted. "Easy? Some of those guys will be in the hospital for weeks."

Shay shrugged. "But none of them are dead, which is more than we can say for anyone else who has tangled with the Silver Ghost. You don't go from chopping heads off and blowing holes in people to not killing a single man in a fight unless you're trying. Trust me. I know. I've been there. No, she let them live on purpose, even if she did beat the shit out of them. It's her sick idea of justice."

"She's not a fucking champion of the people just because she didn't murder a bunch of cops when she got the chance." James glowered.

Peyton took a deep breath and typed a few commands into his computer. "Okay, let's presume it is the alien woman—Erin, or whatever her real name is. What does it all mean, besides her checking out James? She could do all of that without killing a bunch of people in LA and Vegas. Even all that calibration stuff she's been talking about. Why not go to a war zone and do it?"

"It's a challenge to James, maybe?" Heather suggested. "If this is personal, then maybe she's hoping he comes at her, or maybe it's just a way to motivate herself."

James grunted and shrugged. "Doesn't fucking matter. If it *is* her, I know I can win, but we still have to track her down."

Peyton nodded. "What about getting Victoria to do some sort of tracking spell, or maybe even Zoe? I get that Zoe doesn't work for you, but I'm sure Trey could convince her to help." He waggled his eyebrows.

James shook his head. "I don't know if the alien's got access to anti-tracking magic or whatever, but according to the cops, the PDA can't find her. The only chance anyone would have at this point would be if they had a physical focus, and no one's found anything like that. Cops have confirmed they've got shit; no DNA, no residue, nothing."

"How can she leave nothing?"

James shrugged. "The nanites probably self-destruct if they get separated from the main body. I saw that in Canada."

Shay sighed. "The only thing I'm concerned about is that it's actually her and not another nanoform."

"Doesn't matter. If it is, I can beat that shit easy. We need to keep up our non-magical search. If she's not tele-porting or portaling, that means she has to get from place to place somehow. We just need to find her when she's doing that."

"Lots of ways to get from place to place without being seen." Peyton shrugged. "Like she could be using under-ground tunnels to get to her targets."

Shay ran her tongue inside her cheek, her eyes narrowed. "Yeah, she could." She snapped her fingers. "I'll contact Harry and have his little gang keep an eye out. They see a lot of weird stuff that other people miss, and if the Silver Ghost is using tunnels, they'll find out. Just need to make it very clear they should stay the hell away from her. If she's willing to go after cops, I'm not confident she won't cut down teens working legally questionable jobs."

James frowned. "I should reinforce that for Trey. I don't think he'd go after her since she's a level five, but since he doesn't know about any of this alien shit, he also doesn't know how dangerous she might be."

Heather sighed. "So where does that leave us?"

"We have a good idea who the enemy is now, which means we at least know what's motivating her."

Heather shrugged. "But does that even help?"

James chuckled and nodded. "Damn right it helps. Because we know her end goal, and her end target." He pointed with a thumb at his chest. "Me. We still need to push on this to find her before she hurts someone else, but if it *is* the alien woman, there's no way she's going to wander off before taking a shot at me. That's probably what all that calibration and testing is for. She's getting ready to take me down."

Shay rubbed her temples. "I wish I'd had some idea who she was when I met Erin. I could have followed her to her car and slit her throat. Then it'd all be over."

"It'll all be over soon enough." James slammed a fist into his palm. "As soon as we find her."

CHAPTER THIRTEEN

Trey glanced at Victoria in the passenger seat of his F-350 as they barreled down the 95. The pale redhead looked out the window with a pensive expression on her face. He couldn't tell if she was bored or worried.

Vic can't be that worried about the Ghost, can she? Ain't never seen her all that scared, even when those level fours got the drop on her.

"You worried?" Trey prodded.

The witch shook her head. "No, just thinking. You're not the only one who's going through life changes, you know? I'm still wrapping my mind around being a bounty hunter working for James Brownstone, of all people. Even if I've been doing it for a little while now, it doesn't always feel real. Maybe chasing after some mysterious vigilante rather than the Mafia and gang garbage we tend to go after is making me think about it more."

Trey nodded. "Regretting joining up? Want to go back to bodyguard work?"

"Actually, no." Victoria furrowed her brow. "The thing

is, at the end of the day, I get to practice my skills, and I know the people we go after are trash. You saw the kind of scum I sometimes worked for as a bodyguard. Yeah, I could have been choosier, but in the end, it's nice to have a job where I make good money and I'm not making the world a worse place."

"I hear that." Trey clucked his tongue. "I used to think I was the king of badasses, leading my boys around the neighborhood. I tried to keep shit from getting too bad, but you don't have a gang if you never do nothing illegal. I forbade pimping and shit like that, but I don't know. If we hadn't ended up joining up with the big man, we might have gone down a deep hole we couldn't dig our way out of. End up like real garbage, not just some boys protecting their neighborhood."

Victoria glanced his way. "And you're not mad at James over Shorty dying?"

"Fuck, no." Trey sighed. "You have to understand. When you grow up as a gangbanger in the hood, you don't think you're gonna ever grow old. Not because you think you're immortal, but because you think you'll get your ass shot before that. You either leave the lifestyle by choice and become an accountant or some shit, or you leave in a box they put six feet in the ground. Eat, drink, and be mother-fucking merry, for tomorrow you may die. That's what it means to be a gang member." He shook his head. "But those deaths ain't gonna be some epic shit defending the Earth against crazy-ass Oriceran assholes who are sucking people's souls out and shit. Dying is a punk-ass drive-by in a bullshit territory dispute."

"But Shorty's still dead, and he died young."

Trey nodded slowly. "He died saving my life. He died fighting the Council. His death had more meaning than it would have, and you know what? There ain't no one who survives life, so the next best thing is to make sure we go down in a way that means something. I don't want to die young, but if I do, I want my death to mean something more than dying to determine who can deal drugs on what street corner."

Victoria shook her head. "I don't know. I guess I want to die old in my bed in my sleep."

"Picked the wrong career paths for that shit."

The witch laughed. "I also want a little excitement. Guess there's a conflict there. Do you regret your past at all?"

Trey sighed. "I don't know if I regret that shit or not. James ain't ever made us feel bad about being ex-bangers, but then I see how much prouder Nana is of me. Makes me feel good, you know what I'm saying?"

Victoria nodded. "I can understand that. My parents are both healers. They aren't pleased with the general combat bent of my magic. It's not like we never talk or anything, but it's really kind of an occasional holiday thing, and I don't talk about my work with them."

A comfortable silence spread between the two of them, Trey concentrating on the road and Victoria watching the traffic.

Trey cleared his throat. "You think I should have told Zoe all the shit that's going on before she went back to LA? I mean, sure, we're gonna be living here full time soon, but I kind of feel like I'm lying to her by not telling her about all this. I don't know if that makes me a bitch or not. I ain't ever dated a woman quite like her, and I don't always know what to make of her."

Victoria shrugged. "I haven't met her, but everything you've told me about her makes her sound like a very powerful and far older witch than me, even if she specializes in a less flashy type of magic. She probably has her own secrets—tons of them. Don't worry about it too much." She frowned. "We just need to catch the Silver Ghost, since Brownstone's so obsessed. Then it won't matter for you, and we can all go back to making easy money. I'm surprised he cares so much, to be honest."

"He's always been tight with the 5-0, even though they haven't always liked him, and Maria's one of his right-hand women now, so I'm sure she's filling his ear with righteous vengeance shit." Trey shrugged and changed lanes. "But the big man points me somewhere, I say, 'How fast do you want me to get there, sir?'" He grinned.

"Need some damn leads, though." Victoria furrowed her brow. "Did Kathy give you anything useful? I meant to ask you earlier."

"She's trying, but I don't know how useful the shit she gave me is. A few attacks locally, Mafia types mostly, a few gangbangers, but they don't have any witnesses like they do in LA, so people ain't a hundred percent sure if it is the Silver Ghost or just people using the rumors of the Ghost to settle scores."

"Isn't that counterproductive? How do you show your strength if you're hiding behind the rumor of someone else?"

Trey shrugged. "Deplete enough of the enemy, it ain't much matter if they know it's you, because when you finish them off, they'll still be gone. Fewer threats mean fewer losses on your side."

Victoria rolled her eyes. "You do know you're a bounty hunter and not an ancient Roman or Chinese general?"

"Hey, I always respect the wisdom of the ancients. You don't end up with an empire or helping an empire take over if you don't know what you're doing."

"Doesn't help us with our current enemy." Victoria chuckled. "I think one thing I preferred about being a bodyguard was that you didn't have to look for people. Your clients always wanted you around, and the people who wanted your clients dead would show without you asking them to, but this rolling around town hoping to get lucky stuff is obnoxious. This isn't exactly Ye Olde Village of Vegas. The chance we'll randomly run into her might as well be zero."

Trey grinned. "Yeah, but that's the thing about fishing, you know what I'm saying? If you just toss a line in, maybe you get shit, but you have to have the right bait."

The witch side-eyed him. "You spend a lot of time fishing? You don't really strike me as the type."

"Nah, but I've seen movies and shit where they be fishing." Trey pulled into the HOV lane and sped up. "When I was talking to Kathy this morning, I figured, why use her just to hear things when she can also say things?"

"What do you mean?"

Trey offered Victoria his best shit-eating grin. "I told her to put the word out that the Brownstone Agency and Trey motherfucking Garfield in particular are looking for the Silver Ghost, and if we catch the Silver Ghost, we're more than willing to pass along a nice chunk of change to whatever snitching sonsofbitches sell her out, and if anyone happens to personally know the Ghost, they can whisper in that crazy bitch's ear that she can come at me anytime."

Victoria frowned. "Wait, Brownstone said to not engage; to leave her to him. She's a level five. You're not worried about that?"

Trey snorted. "Whatever. I got my motherfucking gloves, and you got your badass witch magic, and this bitch works alone, which makes shit easier. We can take on the Silver Ghost without the big man. We might have to, because he might not be able to get here in time even if we spot her. We just gonna let her get the fuck away? I ain't down with that."

"A level five, though?" Victoria raised an eyebrow. "I'm a pretty tough bitch, but I'm still worried about that."

Trey rolled his eyes. "She ain't no real level five."

"I've got a bounty notice that says otherwise."

Trey shook his head. "Nah, you don't understand. She's a level five because the 5-0 are embarrassed that she handed their asses to them. I'm not saying I'm happy about that. I met Weber, and he's all right for a cop, but they all are freaking out because she hurt some of theirs. No one said shit about her being a level five when she was killing gang members, you know what I'm saying? We've only had trouble in the past because we were talking multiple level fours. A single level five is different shit, and like I said, we can do this as long as it's just her. No one has said shit about the Ghost having backup."

Victoria frowned. "I'm still not sure."

"Nah, check this shit out. She's been beating up gang

members and a few gangsters here and there. Surprising them. Yeah, yeah, she beat the 25K in their place, but if she had a decent magic shield, that accounts for that." Trey patted his chest. "Give me a bulletproof vest and my gloves and I can take bullets too, and I ain't no level five. I probably could have taken out those bitches if I got the drop on them. Do you think you'd be level five, even with your magic and the ability to bounce off bullets?"

The witch shook her head. "What about the AET? Armor, rifles, and anti-magic bullets?"

Trey grinned. "That's the shit, though. Think about AET. They are all normal-ass humans like me. They ain't PDA. They ain't even the military, and they ain't got shit for magic. They're not magic; they're just anti-magic. The Silver Ghost gets the drop on them, and they try their guns out and then realize that shit ain't working too late, and that's how she schools them. You and me, though... We ain't just got anti-magic, we've got actual magic—my artifact and your general badass witchiness." He glanced her way. "All the information we got ain't said shit about her going after a magical criminal, right? Just gangsters with swords and that kind of shit. That's got to mean something."

Victoria nodded, a thoughtful expression on her face. "That's a good point. Not like there aren't magical bounties and criminals to go after, especially in LA."

"Exactly, which means she's afraid to do it. I know she's got that regeneration, but if we can just knock her out or tie her up somehow, that shit won't matter." Trey chuckled. "Yeah, we can take down the Silver Ghost. You and me, together, I know we can. We're a badass team, Vic."

A hungry look appeared in the witch's eyes, and she licked her lips. "I'll admit I do like the idea of a challenge, and you make a compelling argument. Aren't you worried about going against Brownstone?"

Trey shook his head. "At the end of the day, the big man cares about results, not rules. He ain't gonna blow his stack if we take this bitch down for him. It's one less thing he needs to do. He can sit at home, play with his dog, cook barbeque, and save himself for the next Council who shows up and shit like that."

"You're sure you're willing to take on a level five?"

"Damn right. At least a single level five. We know a lot about this Silver Ghost, and she ain't summoning no demons or frying people's brains with her eyes. Probably don't have a shield, just regeneration. Bitch can't even fly, which means we're on even terms." Trey's hands tightened on the wheel. "I'm just saying, we try if we get the chance. From everything the big man's heard, he'll hit her in LA before we find her in Vegas."

Victoria leaned back in her seat, silent for a good thirty seconds before responding, "Why are you so hellbent on this? Is this some sort of big-dick thing?"

Trey shook his head. "I've been thinking a lot lately about the move and what it represents. How things have changed, both with my training and my gear. I need to step up my game, and that means pushing myself. A man needs to know his limits if he wants to push past them. That's the only way he can grow. That's what James, Staff Sergeant, and Marcus Aurelius all taught me."

Victoria shrugged. "Fine. I've got your back if she shows

up, but if we take her down ourselves, we're getting the bulk of that bounty."

Trey laughed. "If money is your only standard, then consider that, by your lights, someone who loses their nose does not suffer any harm."

The witch blinked. "Huh?"

"Marcus Aurelius said that."

Victoria snorted. "Easy thing for an emperor to say. Let's just find ourselves a witch; we can figure out the stoic crap later."

Trey smiled. "Fine by me."

CHAPTER FOURTEEN

James looked back and forth in the narrow hallway before knocking on the apartment door. He wasn't expecting anyone suspicious, but checking around before meeting with an informant was a good general policy.

No obvious cameras. Good way to meet people at home without someone knowing what's up. Harry and his friends have good instincts. Then again, no one would ever know what happened if someone came in here and did something to them.

Shay looked down at the smooth carpet and chuckled. "Nice. Not five star, but a big step up from living in tunnels. It's funny how far all these kids have come since I met Lily."

"That's on you."

"What do you mean?"

"You helped them all, you know," James replied. "If you hadn't started training Lily and paying her, those kids would have stayed tunnel rats for years, running around stealing to survive. Now, because of Lily's success and the money, they've got a good business going, and they have a chance at a future that doesn't end with gangsters killing them because they took the wrong shit."

Did Harry hear me? He's the one who set up the meeting time.

James knocked again.

"I wasn't trying to help them. I was trying to wring something useful out of Lily. Helping them was incidental." Shay shrugged. "It was self-interest, not altruism."

"You could have cut Lily loose at any time, but you didn't. You even helped her when she fucked up." James chuckled. "Self-interest? I could say the same thing about Trey and the guys. I'm just lazy and don't want to be bothered with low-level bounties. Self-interest and altruism don't have to be separate things."

Light footsteps sounded from the other side. The locks clicked, and the door opened.

Finally.

"Sorry. I was on the phone checking on something when you knocked," Harry offered.

"Not a big deal."

He looked old for his age, but that only meant he looked like an older teenager. He offered a nod to both Shay and James before gesturing to a tattered blue sectional sofa by a matching recliner in an otherwise barren living room. There wasn't even a tv on the wall.

Huh. I guess you can take a guy out of the tunnels, but that doesn't mean he's going to get rid of those tunnel-living instincts anytime soon. Not that living simply is that bad a thing. I would have been less pissed when they blew up my house if I'd had fewer things.

James grunted and headed over to the sofa to take a seat. Shay sat beside him. Unlike James, she'd been to the place before, and her face betrayed no hint of surprise at the minimalist decor.

"Your message said you had some information," James rumbled. "I'm guessing I'd be too damned lucky if you already found out where the Silver Ghost lives."

Harry moved over to the recliner to sit. "Yeah, still working on that, but it's not like we've got nothing for you. First off, a few simple things. My guys asked around and found a few witnesses the cops hadn't. I can a hundred percent verify that she can't teleport or portal. She jumps like crazy and climbs like a damned spider, though. She runs fast, but it's not, like, superhumanly fast."

Shay nodded. "That's consistent with everything we've heard. That's still annoying enough, but at least that means James can fight her on equal mobility terms."

Harry shrugged. "As for her moving around using the tunnels? I really, really doubt it. We've asked a lot of tunnel rats, and no one has seen her. If anything, the tunnels have been super-quiet lately, and people have been paying a lot more attention this year in general because of all the stuff that happened with that Council bastard."

"Maybe she's traveling in disguise when she's under-ground," James suggested. "To look non-threatening, like just another homeless woman. That kind of shit."

"Why bother? It's not like AET's going to hit the tunnels. They'd get lost down there in five minutes." Harry shook his head, a defiant look on his face. "I'm telling you that she's not using the tunnels. I'd bet you a thousand dollars she's not. I'm confident as both an information broker and a former tunnel rat."

Shay frowned. "Then she might just be straight-up turning invisible. Maybe she's trying to make sure no one near the kill sites knows she has the power? She's got to be living somewhere if she's not teleporting in, and I'm guessing that somewhere is in Los Angeles County."

"Your guess is as good as mine." Harry smiled. "We did pick up an interesting tidbit from someone who used to work at the Kowloon. They're illegal, and have kept away from the cops because they're afraid of getting deported."

James nodded. "What did they say?"

Harry leaned forward, eagerness on his face. "One of Johnny Lee's guys came in an hour before the attack, all busted up. Obviously had been in a fight and lost. This person overheard the guy say something like, 'She's coming.'"

"So they definitely knew she was coming."

Shay patted one of her sheaths in her jacket pocket. "That explains why they were armed up."

James furrowed his brow. "If she didn't show up for an hour, she probably let the guy go on purpose. It must have been to work their nerves. I've done that shit."

Shay shrugged. "So have I." She looked at Harry. "Hear about anything like that with any of the other incidents, such as the gang members she killed in Wilmington? I wonder if it's a change in her behavior."

Harry shook his head. "Nope. That's the only incident I've heard of where she clearly warned people beforehand, unless you want to count the warning she gave the cops before she beat them down."

"No offense, but this shit doesn't help us." James let out a low growl. "We need something else useful. Patterns. Probable locations. Additional evidence. The cops have some incidents, but they don't know everything. For all we know, she's been killing people the cops don't even know about.

"At least in the case of two hitmen, that's true." Harry pulled up his phone and tapped it a few times before holding it up to show them a map with a couple of red dots in Hollywood. "Cops don't know about these incidents, but we've got two strong eyewitnesses who saw the Silver Ghost go through the window and kill the guys inside. They didn't report it to the cops because the witnesses were connected to the Russian Mafia, as were the victims. The Russians moved the bodies before the cops found them. Word is the Russians are holding back for now, waiting to see what you do about it."

James frowned. "Me?"

"Yeah. The minute that level five went out, everyone, high and low, started talking about how they figured you'd be the one to end this."

"I've seen that as well on my old dark web haunts," Shay explained.

James shrugged. "Good to be popular, I guess."

Shay frowned. "Forget that crap for now. When were these killings?"

"A week ago."

"This further proves that for all her posturing and the shit she said to the cops, the Silver Ghost isn't going out of her way to advertise her kills. I mean, she could be trying to put the fear into the LA underworld, but she's not really bothering." She gave James a curious look. "Makes me think that's not her main objective, but I guess it doesn't matter as long as we find her."

Yeah, I know what you're getting at. This is more about training for her than doing much about the criminals in the city. Don't doubt that, just don't know what to do with it.

Harry smiled. "Anyway, I've got everybody looking and asking around. People tell us things they wouldn't tell the cops, let alone James." He shrugged, an apologetic look on his face. "No offense, it's just that you are kind of a force of nature, and a lot of people on the wrong side of the law are extra worried right now that you might take a page from the Silver Ghost's book."

James frowned. "What the fuck? What do you mean?"

Shay's expression darkened, but she didn't say anything.

The boy sighed and shrugged. "Everyone knows what you did to the Harriken, James. I mean, even people not connected in any way to the underworld know. There are Scourge of Harriken websites."

"First of all, I didn't set those up," James growled. "Second, they fucked with my dog. People who fuck with my dog, my friends, or my family get fucked up in return. Simple policy, and the Harriken didn't learn the lesson. That's why they're gone now."

Harry threw up his hands. "I know, I know. Not saying I miss them. I barely dealt with them, and I still think they were grade-A assholes. The world's a better place without them, but a lot of people are thinking, 'Well, if the Silver Ghost just kills whoever she wants without bounties, what if Brownstone starts too?' And they've started to make plans with that in mind."

James grunted. "I'm only doing this because of the bounty and because the cops asked me to. I'm not going to become a vigilante. That shit takes too much work and makes life more complicated. Everyone I've ever fucked with in my entire life either had a bounty or fucked with me or someone I cared about."

Shay snickered. "You know what, that's probably true. I'm more likely to become a vigilante than James, so people can stop wetting their pants."

"I know. I'm just saying, is all." Harry leaned forward. "And I wanted you to know the general mood on the streets, not just among the high-end gangsters and stuff. The point is, you catching the Silver Ghost isn't just good for the cops, it's good for everybody. It'll defuse a bomb that's close to going off. The last thing LA needs is for the entire underworld to lose their damned minds over Brownstone...again."

"Could make money off bets." Shay shrugged. "Another Great Brownstone Hunt or Chase or whatever the hell Tyler called it."

James grunted. "Doesn't matter. I'm ending this shit before it gets that far. The Silver Ghost can't hide forever, and now she's got everyone looking for her. She should have stuck to killing guys in alleys."

Shay turned to Harry. "We need your help to do this. There's got to be some pattern to what the Ghost is doing. If she were teleporting, I could buy that it was random, but she's choosing to go to specific places, which means she has particular reasons and pre-selected targets. We need to figure out how she's picking those targets." She gestured to Harry's phone. "I think you

realize that, too. It's why you're carefully tracking locations on maps."

Harry nodded. "Yes, but we haven't found anything.
She's been all over the metro area, and the neighborhood
seems random by night." His eyes widened. "That *is* one
thing we've been able to confirm. She only attacks at
night."

"Better to hide," James suggested. "Not that surprising."

"Or maybe her powers don't work in the sun." Shay
shrugged. "If she's using some sort of invisibility technique,
it might be too obvious during the day. That limits her
hours of attack, but we still need the next location."

"Yeah. Maybe there's something else connecting them,
like they're all the same distance from a central point. I've
found guys before looking at that sort of thing."

Harry shook his head. "We've looked at that, but I
honestly don't see any pattern. It all looks like random
choices. I mean, it's not like I've tried to compare to the
number of bagel shops or whatever, but I've tried to look at
everything obvious that concerns distance, location, and
that sort of thing."

"Coordinates," Shay murmured, looking down. She
lifted her head and locked eyes with the teen info broker.
"Get me the coordinates for every incident you can. It's not
that I don't believe in you guys, but we have access to
major data crunchers who might be able to use an algorithm or something to pick out more information, even if
it is something as stupid as the number of local bagel
shops. We're close." She nodded with a frown. "I can feel it.
I can smell it. All my instincts tell me that. This bitch can't
hide completely. We just need to put together the puzzle

pieces that everyone's found: you, the cops and our info specialists."

"Fine," Harry replied. "I'll send you all the information we have, but we can't a hundred percent guarantee that it's going to be the exact location of every incident, only close. It's not like we run around with drones. Just people."

Shay grinned. "Sometimes close enough works. Like with grenades. Or nukes."

Harry chuckled. "Planning to drop a nuke on her?"

"Nah, something better." Shay nodded at James. "Him."

CHAPTER FIFTEEN

Trey wrinkled his nose as he stepped into the dive bar. Even when he'd been working the streets as a gang member, he'd always held himself to a higher standard than a lot of the trash around him. A man had to respect himself and how he presented himself, after all, or no one else would.

Don't matter much. Just here to get a little information. The dry cleaning will get the smell out later.

He ignored the hostile glares coming his way. Probably a quarter of the men in the room had a bounty, but he wasn't there for them. If they wanted to be stupid and come at him, it'd be their own damned fault when he put them down.

The bounty hunter continued through the room toward a back table and his target for today: Anthony. The old man was always easy to pick out with his bad spray tan and ill-fitting suits.

Trey stopped at the informant's table. "You should take

your suit to a motherfucking tailor, Anthony. I know you ain't so poor you can't afford that shit."

The informant looked up at Trey with a smile and shrugged. "Maybe it's just part of my unique charm."

"You ain't got no charm, that's for damned sure." Trey pulled out a chair and sat. "But you did tell me you got some information on the Ghost, and I've got some money dying to leave me and go to you, so why don't you make us both happy?"

Anthony leaned forward with a smirk. "You serious right now, Garfield?"

"When have you ever known me not to be serious when I show up to talk to you, Anthony?" Trey snorted. "You said you have information, so fucking spill already."

"I don't know where the Silver Ghost is, but I do know what people are saying." Anthony sniffed and scratched his nose. "They're saying she isn't real."

Trey laughed. "So who killed all those 25K and all the other people she's laid out? What, they committed suicide?"

Anthony pointed at him. "I'll tell you what the local Mafia thinks. They think the Silver Ghost shit is just a scam to scare people and cover things up. They think some of you Brownstone boys have gotten a little trigger-happy, and you're killing people on the side."

"Most of our bounties ain't dead or alive." Trey frowned. "Best case for killing a non-dead-or-alive bounty is half the bounty, and that's the *best* case. Why the fuck would we do that? We're in this shit for the money."

"Hey, personally, I don't believe that shit." Anthony sat up and shrugged. "If there's one thing I've learned from dealing with you, Garfield, it's that you Brownstone boys are just like your boss. You're all about making a big show to scare people, not hiding and skulking. And it's like you said—what do you get out of it?"

Trey frowned. "This shit ain't useful to me. Why should I pay you for this?"

"Because it's a warning. The Silver Ghost isn't the only person you have to worry about. Word on the street is that people are thinking about a little payback to make it clear that the Brownstone Agency can't do what they want to whoever they want." Anthony sighed. "I, of course, am a neutral party in all this, but I figured you should know. You should watch your back until this Silver Ghost shit is sorted out, Garfield. I'd hate to lose a good source of income."

Trey chuckled and pulled out his phone. He initiated a TrollCoin payment to Anthony and slipped his phone back into his pocket. He didn't need the address information. They did this all the time.

"I'll try not to die and force you to get more dishonest work, Anthony." Trey stood and adjusted his lapels. "But it's going to be a sad day for any motherfuckers who come after me. I ain't the man I once was."

Trey sighed about ten minutes later when he looked in his rearview mirror. He wasn't sure if he would have noticed the tail as easily without Anthony's warning, but the black Lincoln following him wasn't trying to be subtle.

"Thanks, Anthony. I might actually owe you one, but

too bad Vic isn't with me. It'd be a nice warmup for the Silver Ghost."

Trey slowed and changed lanes, thinking about his options. He didn't want to lead them all the way back to the loft. If they had any explosives with them, they might hit the building, and that would be a headache for everyone.

A little evasive driving on the highway might lose them, but that risked damage to his beloved baby—his F-350. As much as Trey respected the big man, he let his truck get damaged too often, and this was one time Trey didn't want to follow in James Brownstone's footsteps.

"Okay," Trey mumbled to himself. "Not gonna be a bitch and lead them to the police, but if I try too much bullshit on the road, not only do I risk the truck, but I also risk other people getting hurt. Guess there's only one obvious option."

Trey looked back and forth, seeking a relatively deserted parking lot. He'd learned his lesson about fighting around cars the expensive way.

Several more minutes passed before he spotted an abandoned movie theater coming up on his right. He took the exit a little too hard, earning a honk from a car behind him, but once he turned into the parking lot, they continued on.

Trey slowed the truck to a stop and slipped on his enchanted gloves after putting his vehicle in Park. He was already wearing his bulletproof vest. There was no way he'd walk into the kind of place Anthony liked to frequent without it.

The Lincoln pulled into the parking lot, and Trey stepped out of his truck and jogged a few yards away from it.

Those motherfuckers better not use a rocket launcher or some shit like that.

Trey waited, his arms crossed, as the Lincoln slowed and stopped about ten yards away. The dark-tinted windows denied him a view of whoever was inside, but everything about the car screamed Mafia to him.

He tapped his foot impatiently, and a good minute passed before all four doors of the car opened and four large men in dark suits and ties stepped out.

At least these bitches are dressing with class. None of this tracksuit-and-chains bullshit.

Trey frowned. "Can I help you, gentlemen?"

One of the men stepped forward, a smile on his face that didn't reach his eyes. "I just want to make sure of something first. You're Trey Garfield, right?" He nodded toward the truck. "I can't imagine there are a lot of guys of your description driving around in some old piece of shit like that."

Trey's face twitched. "Please don't disrespect my truck, and I won't disrespect you."

The man grinned. "Touchy, touchy."

"But yes, I'm Trey Garfield of the Brownstone Agency." Trey gave the man a feral grin. "And who might you be?"

The man adjusted his tie. "We represent local *family* interests."

There we go. Knew they were Mafia bitches.

"Oh, I see. It's good to be a family man. Lots of loyalty

and shit. I can respect that. Any particular family you represent?"

"That's not important," the mobster replied. "The important thing is all this Silver Ghost shit."

Trey chuckled. "Now, there's a point we agree on. If you know anything about the Silver Ghost, there's a reward in it for you. If this is some shit where you think we made it up, I guarantee you're wrong."

The mobster's smile grew. "You see, here's the thing. We've got a different opinion than some. I don't know if the Silver Ghost is some crazy Oriceran bitch who watched too many vigilante movies or if she's just a nasty bedtime story people tell each other at night." He pointed at Trey. "I do know, though, that you've been making a lot of noise about her."

Trey shrugged. "Big man wants her in a bad way. Level five, you know. And the big man don't like people who hurt cops."

"If this was just Brownstone, we could tolerate that." The mobster's smile finally vanished. "No one in Vegas is stupid enough to go up against Brownstone, not like some of those dumb fuckers in Los Angeles. Californians, am I right?" He shrugged and grinned at his friends.

They all laughed.

Trey didn't laugh, but he didn't frown either. He was going to play it cool and let them escalate the situation. If James questioned him later, he wanted it clear that he wasn't picking unnecessary fights and making things *complicated*.

"Yeah, lots of crazy fuckers in Los Angeles," he replied. "Not gonna deny that, but what's your point? If no one in

Vegas is stupid enough to go up against Brownstone, then why are you here talking to me now?"

The mobster shook his head. "Well, that's the thing, isn't it? You're not Brownstone. You might work for him, but you're not him, and he's not here most of the time. You are."

Trey nodded. "True enough, and?"

"The point is, we can tolerate it when Brownstone comes around here and throws his weight around." The mobster shrugged. "Just kind of the price of doing business. You prepare for the hurricane, you know? You don't bitch about it. But you? You're not him. You're just some piece-of-shit gangbanger wannabe acting like Brownstone."

Trey took a deep breath and slowly let it out. "Now, see, there you go. I'm here trying to keep my temper and all that shit, and you're disrespecting me after I went out of my way to show you respect. Now, does that sound fair?"

The men all pulled out brass knuckles and slipped them on.

The lead mobster smiled. "Don't worry, Garfield. We're not going to kill you. We're not dumb enough to kill a guy who works for Brownstone, but we've got to make a point to you and all these people who aren't Brownstone that you can only hide behind your daddy so much. We still rule this town."

Trey looked at the men and nodded. "Fair enough. No one pulled any guns, so that means I don't have to pull a gun. We can keep this all nice and fair."

The four mobsters advanced, and Trey shook out his hands before raising his fists.

"You smug bastard," the lead mobster replied. "We might have let you run away with your tail between your legs, but now you're going to feel some serious pain. Probably going to have to break something to make our point."

"Less talk, more walk, bitch." Trey grinned. "Show me the strength of family ties."

Two of the men rushed forward. Apparently, they were smart enough to not try to take him one at a time. Too bad they weren't smart enough to avoid attacking him at all.

Trey delivered a hard right hook to one, his gloved fist slamming into the man's head. His target spun several times before collapsing to the ground. The other man threw a quick jab, but the bounty hunter blocked the attack and replied with a headbutt.

The mobster stumbled back, gritting his teeth, blood spurting from his nose.

Trey advanced and threw two quick jabs, one to the stomach and the other to the head. The man collapsed in a heap, moaning.

The bounty hunter shook out his hands. "You see, that's your problem, bitches. You should have asked around more about me before you took me on, and then you would have avoided getting all embarrassed and causing trouble you didn't need to."

The remaining enforcer stepped in front of the lead mobster and pulled a knife.

Trey sighed. "Damn, now why did you have to go and do that?" He gestured for the man to attack. "Come on, little man. Let's see what you've got."

The mobster charged, and Trey let the man stab him. His vest wasn't much use against blades, but it slowed the attack enough that by the time it hit his strengthened skin, the only thing he felt was a sting. The mobster grinned down at the knife, obviously waiting for blood to well up. His grin disappeared after a few seconds, and he looked up.

Trey waved to him and slugged him hard in the face. The mobster's head snapped back, and he collapsed to the ground, his eyes rolling up.

"Just you and me now, bitch," Trey sang.

The lead mobster whipped out his gun and pointed it at Trey. "You sonofabitch. What the hell?"

Trey stared at him. Depending on where he was hit, even with the gloves, he wouldn't escape injury, but if the man didn't kill him with one shot, Trey could survive with the help of a healing potion. The thought quashed any fear.

A quick rush could disarm the man, but beating him down then wouldn't be good enough. It might convince the mob to come at him again in the future with more men. No, Trey needed to demolish the man's very *soul* to win and make sure no Mafia bastards ever came at him again.

Trey clucked his tongue. "Like I said, we started this all very polite-like, especially on my end, and then you guys decided to come at me. Out of respect for the fact that you didn't pull a gun immediately, I didn't go for a gun." He held up his hands. "And look, the thing is, I don't want any particular trouble with family men other than the guys with bounties. The way I see it, if one of your guys is enough of a dumbass to get tagged with a bounty, he's fair game, you know what I'm saying?"

The mobster's face twitched. "I'm the one with a fucking gun on you."

Trey snorted. "And your friend there just stabbed me,

and I didn't even blink. Don't that make you think just a little bit that maybe, just maybe, I'm out of your league? I could have wasted all your asses with ease, but there's a couple of reasons I ain't doing that." He held up a finger. "First of all, I ain't remembering you all having any boun- ties on your asses, let alone dead-or-alive bounties.' He held up a second finger. "Second, I'm like you. I'm a family man, and I belong to a family headed by one major badass, James Brownstone. He ain't want me stirring up trouble. Out of respect for you and him, let's just end this shit. I'm gonna walk over there and get in my truck and drive off. If you want to live, you'll put your gun away and help your guys back into your car and drive off." He scowled at the man. "Or you can try to shoot me, and then I'll be forced to kill all your asses to make a point. You'll be dead, and I won't have any money to show for it, and I'll waste a lot of time talking to the cops. Why don't you save us both the trouble?"

He locked eyes with the other man. After ten seconds, the mobster's arm began to dip. A few more seconds passed before the mobster let his gun drop to his side.

"You're tougher than they say," the mobster muttered.

"Well, I learned from the best." Trey grinned. No reason to let the asshole know about his artifact. "Look, you may think I'm an uppity bitch, but the truth is, the big man *might* kill you if you cause trouble, and I *might* come after you if you have a bounty, but the Silver Ghost is real, and she's going around killing people just because they are crooks. If you really want to do something to help your family, let them know to pass on any information about the Ghost. Like I said, money in it for you."

The mobster stared at Trey, his mouth open in disbelief.

Trey waved and walked back to his truck. He opened the door and slipped inside.

The mobster was still standing there, gun at his side, when Trey pulled away.

CHAPTER SIXTEEN

P eyton licked his lips and clicked his mouse.

Okay, let's do this thing.

His eyes moved back and forth as he looked over the collated coordinate data Shay had sent to him and Heather, along with the nature of the victims and the times of the incidents. A few more keystrokes and a map with various colored dots appeared on his second monitor.

There's got to be a pattern here. Just because a bunch of teens couldn't find it doesn't mean it isn't there. There's a reason the Silver Ghost chose these victims and these locations, so what is it?

He frowned and looked at Heather's webcam picture. Judging by the deep frown on her face, she wasn't finding much either.

Peyton entered a few more commands to initiate additional analyses.

"I'm just not seeing it," he muttered. "It looks like random noise. I've tried to run a bunch of pattern-matching algorithms, and I'm not getting any decent fits. It's like there's no pattern at all."

Heather shook her head and sighed. "Same here. If there's some sort of time- or location-based pattern to this, it's not something I can identify through any of the analyses I've run. I've got a few general-purpose matching algorithms running, and I'm waiting for results on those."

Peyton furrowed his brow. "Yeah, me too. Sounds like a good plan. I mean, even if she is an alien, it's not like she's totally inscrutable, right? I mean, she lived on Earth for ten years as a human and fit in with humans. She's probably got the equivalent of a better education and technology. There's no reason to think she has some master ability to plan attacks that come off as completely random to us lower lifeforms, right?"

Osiris meowed from beneath the computer desk, perhaps offering his thoughts on who the true masters of Earth should be.

She's not a mouse. You won't be much help.

After a few seconds of intense typing, Heather shrugged. "We don't know if this Silver Ghost is the alien, and if she is, we can't really say one way or another. I mean, to be honest, judging by the Oricerans, different intelligent species think all sorts of different ways."

"But she's not some weird rock monster or flame sprite or some crap like that." Peyton shook his head. "She's humanoid, so that's got to mean she's at least somewhat like us in thought, right?"

"We don't know that she's humanoid. We only know the shape she's presented to Shay. For all we know, she's an android of some sort. That might explain the appearance."

Peyton snorted. "Android who rants about evil and monsters? She doesn't sound like an emotionless machine."

Heather tapped a few keys. "Who says alien machines have no emotions? Assuming she's not a machine, she might have some really foreign way of thinking or access to advanced math techniques or something else we can't begin to understand. The point is, we don't know one way or another, so we can't make any assumptions. The only thing we can do is keep plugging away at the data and trying to find something useful. Anything else is just a lot of pointless guessing. It might be fun as a thought experiment, but it won't help us track down the Silver Ghost."

Peyton sighed and slumped in his chair. It was hard to find fault with Heather's logic.

"Maybe there's something else we can do. Something more proactive than looking through data."

Heather frowned. "Like what?"

"I was wondering about us sending up like an entire fleet of drones. Just coating the city, and looking for where we lose signal—like a passive detection grid. If we have enough, maybe we can narrow it down to a certain area and have James go there."

Heather frowned. "There's no way we could coordinate that many drones without running into other trouble. It'd be too much of a risk of leading them back to either you or me."

"We could mass-hack a bunch of drones to use as a temporary net."

"That's the same problem. We can't guarantee the Ghost will attack on any particular day, and if we take over hundreds of people's drones, someone's going to notice. That's going to cause trouble." Heather shook her head. "And hundreds might not even be enough. We don't have a clear idea on how far her jamming goes. It might take thousands of drones to cover enough area, and that's just not practical." She sucked in a breath. "No, we need to narrow the area down a bit if we're going to give James a chance to find her. There has to be something we're missing; some pattern. We just need to find the right dataset to compare the sightings to or tease out the pattern some other way."

"But isn't the government looking at all this stuff too?" Peyton asked. "I mean, we're both badasses, don't get me wrong, but the FBI has access to analysts, too. They've got to be thinking the same thing."

"They also have a lot more rules about what and where they can go, especially for criminal investigations." Heather nibbled on her lip. "We semi-criminal freelancers can use our freedom to find things they couldn't dream of finding."

"If you say so."

"Have a little confidence. We've both hacked into tons of government systems, and you hacked into servers and landed top-secret Project Nephilim and Ragnarök information—the super-secret alien stuff that's not supposed to exist." Heather grinned and typed a few commands in. "No, I'm not convinced that a bunch of government data analysts can find something better than we can on this job. Yeah, if they threw the whole NSA at it or something, that's one thing, but they're not doing that for a random vigilante in Los Angeles, even a level five. Besides, you're forgetting something important, something that separates us from the FBI."

Peyton furrowed his brow. "What's that?"

"If this *is* Erin, we already beat this bitch once." Heather grinned. "After all, she's the one who got so spooked she faked her own death. Our low-tech primitive human asses beat her, and that was when she had years and billions of dollars to set herself up. She's got to be more vulnerable now, not less, so we can beat her again, especially since she decided to come to our city and mess around."

Peyton bobbed his head. "Shit, you're right." He clicked through a few custom self-learning pattern-matching algorithms and fed them the location and time dataset. "What if it's something ridiculous, though, like she rolls a die to figure out where to go? If it's truly random, there's nothing we can do."

"Truly random means every variable is random, though. If she's pre-selected certain locations or times, then there's still a pattern. We already know she limits herself to attacks at night, for example, so I doubt it is truly random." Heather shook her head. "But if it is, yeah, we're fucked, but I'm having trouble believing a vigilante alien decides her victims by a dice roll or something without any other fundamental pattern. Not only that, she has to know where and who the victims are. It's not like she's just traveling around beating up muggers. She killed those hitmen in their apartments, and they weren't in the middle of a job. No, there's a logic here. Otherwise, it just seems…wrong, somehow. Too weird. Maybe even too human."

"As opposed to an alien who loves classic trucks and barbeque and hot-tempered human women?" Peyton raised a brow. "Our definitions of what might be too human don't stand up to the people we know."

"Okay, you do have me there." Heather laughed. "It sounds ridiculous when you say it that way, though."

"Everything's ridiculous since Oriceran. Keep in mind, they are aliens, too. Just because they're from a magic planet doesn't change that, so it's hard to worry too much about figuring everything out." Peyton shook his head. "Since I took care of my brother, all I worry about is helping my friends. I try to let everything else sort itself out, and you have a kid. I'm guessing he's easy to focus on."

"He is. It's just…" Heather narrowed her eyes and began typing furiously.

Peyton frowned. "Heather?"

She didn't respond. She continued typing, her frown turning into a smile.

"Heather, what is it? What did you find?"

She held up her hand to stop him before returning to typing.

Peyton shrugged and crossed his arms, waiting for her to finish doing whatever she was doing. She must have had a good reason.

Please, please tell me you found something, and not that it correlates perfectly with a particular dice-rolling sequence.

Heather stopped typing and clicked her mouse a few times. "I just sent you a file. Read it over real quick. It'll be easier if you look it over rather than me explaining."

A window popped up along with the icon for the transferred file, and Peyton clicked on the icon. Several labeled rows and columns appeared, with information on the incidents and the location data, but there was an additional column with text in it on the far right he hadn't seen in the previous data.

Peyton clicked on the first row in the far column. The full text of the message popped up in a separate window.

He quickly scanned it. His eyes widened, and then he clicked another message and read it, and then another.

Peyton blinked. "How did you even know to match up the data against these files?"

Heather smiled. "I was trawling local message boards for certain keywords, and my search algorithm kicked back possible matches. I ran a couple of quick follow-up comparisons, and that's what I found. The times and locations match."

"But this…is, seriously?" Peyton shook his head.

"Why not?" Heather grinned. "Puts a new perspective on busybody neighbors."

"If I'm reading this right, it suggests that the Silver Ghost is picking targets through a combination of social media bitching, neighborhood watch boards, and local HOA noise complaints, along with police reports."

Heather nodded. "Exactly. It's not any one of those sources, it's the interplay of them all. The police reports probably form her initial filter, then she follows up with the other sources to pick out targets that might have a more general impact, or whatever you want to call it. The social media probably gives her a good feel for the urgency of the targets."

Peyton grimaced. "It's a good thing I keep to myself, and I'm still coming back from being dead."

Heather chuckled. "Don't you see? This is the key."

"I get that we found the pattern, but how do we use it? It'll get us some probable targets, but it doesn't look like she's going in a particular order or anything. It'll narrow down the number of targets, but it'll still involve James having to somehow be able to drive to anywhere in the greater LA area at a moment's notice. I don't know how practical that is."

"Maybe." Heather smacked her lips. "But we can potentially use these places to lay a trap or something. Now that we know what data sources she's using, if we insert the right data, it'll increase the chance of her going somewhere we want her to go."

Peyton frowned. "She might be too smart for that."

"I don't know. For now, let's just let Shay and James know. They can figure out how to use the information, and we can continue probing things and seeing if we can find more useful stuff."

CHAPTER SEVENTEEN

James stared down at his phone and grunted as he shifted in his recliner. He looked at Shay, who'd just been sent the same information, and waited for her to look up. Her wrinkled brow smoothed out after a minute, and she shook her head before sitting up on the couch.

"Okay, they've cracked the code," Shay murmured. "The thing is, how do we want to use it? Chances are, whatever we do with it, we will potentially only get one shot if the Silver Ghost realizes what we're doing with it."

James shrugged. "It's easy. We just have them plant information that suggests I'm going to go after some piece of shit in a particular location. There's no way she'll resist coming after me if it's the alien."

"Are you sure about that?" Shay frowned. "If she just wanted to come after you, why hasn't she already? It's not like your address is top secret."

"Because she's waiting for the right opportunity. And even if she was willing to beat down the AET, she still tried to warn them off. If she comes after me in the middle of a residential area, she's risking collateral damage, and maybe her warped little conscience won't allow that." James shook his head. "I'm willing to take advantage of that to make sure no one else gets hurt. If she doesn't want to get other people involved, it's fine by me, but if I go somewhere that's empty at a particular time and present a nice juicy target, she'll come. I just need to find a place that will be safe enough for us to fight, but where it makes sense that I might take on a bounty or look for one."

"Okay, that's logical." Shay tapped her lips. "But where?"

"Maybe the Salton Sea. There won't be any collateral damage, and I've fought different people out there."

"You love that place so much, you should build a cabin out there." Shay snorted.

James shrugged. "It's remote, and there's not a lot of people there anymore. It's good for ass-kicking, and it's perfect for this kind of situation."

Shay sighed. "It's also pointless. Everything we've found suggests she's got good land mobility, but no teleporting and no flying. Not only that, she's concerned about being spotted, or she wouldn't bother with jamming and shit like that. There's no way we can guarantee she'd be willing to go all the way out to a place like the Salton Sea." She shook her head. "We need somewhere in the LA or Vegas metro areas, places within easy reach of where she's already been spotted. We could clear out a park or something. The police were the ones who came sniffing for you. They'll agree to help."

James grunted. "I don't want any more cops involved. She's already proven she doesn't give a shit about hurting cops, and if they aren't AET, they might end up getting killed. I've got every reason to believe it's that alien bitch, which means this isn't just a bounty, it's personal. I don't need to drag the police into my personal shit any more than they already have been. Fuck this alien bitch, and fuck the Vax."

"That pushes us back to our same basic question. Where, then?"

"Maybe Chino Hills?" James worked his jaw as he thought over the possibilities. "If I go at night, it shouldn't be a problem."

Shay shook her head. "There have been no Silver Ghost sightings in that area or other areas like that. It's probably still too remote. She's sticking to the city for a reason, even if it's just mobility and hiding, so it's going to need to be in the city proper."

James grunted. "Plenty of abandoned buildings around town. From what we've heard about her abilities, it's not like she's going to blow up a city block."

Shay stared at him. "*You* might, if you get pissed enough."

"Need to make sure there's enough old shit around to blow up, then." James picked up his phone. "I only give a shit about her killing people, not property damage. I can always pay for it." He tapped in a search.

Abandoned locations in metro Los Angeles.

Shay peered at him. "What are you doing?"

"Looking shit up on the internet." James shrugged. "Who knows, maybe they have a good suggestion? Lot of bored people sit around figuring shit like this out."

Shay snickered. "Seriously? You've got two crack hackers, a brilliant girlfriend—if I do say so myself—access to informant networks, police records, and elves, and you're doing an internet search?"

"Despite what you think, sometimes the simplest method is the best." James shrugged. "I found Jessie Rae's from an internet search, and that's one of the best things that has ever happened to me."

"James Brownstone, going through life off what search engines give him." Shay grinned. "That explains so much about you."

He brought up the first link, read through it, and grunted. "Lots of tunnels, but some of those aren't abandoned. Shit, Harry and Lily and all of them were living in that nuclear tunnel. Plus, too many tunnels run under places with lots of people. Plus, I don't want to take her on in some fucking maze where she might escape when I start winning."

A quick tap took him to the next link. More tunnels.

After that, the problem was the definition used by the sites of the word "abandoned" seemed stretched beyond usefulness, including calling locations abandoned that had been left by their original owners and then turned into tourist attractions. Tourists might be annoying, but they didn't deserve to die in an alien-on-alien crossfire.

After a few minutes, James stopped and narrowed his eyes at a link. He tapped it and quickly read the description. "I think I've got a place."

Shay smiled. "All hail the internet. What place is that?"

"Northwest Pacific Hospital. It's been abandoned for years, it's in the general metro area, and people avoid it. Even the homeless, according to this site, because ghosts and other magic shit show up there from time to time.

Apparently, people have been riding the politicians to have PDA show up and do something about it, but they say there's no significant threat to the public, so it's not a good use of resources." James grunted.

"Ghosts can be annoying." Shay shrugged. "But they also have the advantage of being dead already, so it's not like you'll hurt them more if you end up having to blow up the building or some shit. Sounds like a good choice, and there might not even be any ghosts there."

"Now I just have to get her there." James furrowed his brow. "Heather and Peyton can probably do that with the stuff they found."

"If you have them push it too hard, it might bring other people looking to take a shot at you. Just keep that in mind. You don't want a repeat of your pay-per-view surprise."

"I'll go in ready and bonded, and I've got much better control of Whispy now." James snorted. "If anyone else wants to get in the way, I'll fucking knock them to the side. If they're in LA and they haven't bought a fucking clue by now, there isn't anything anyone can do for them." He nodded. "Yeah, time to have Heather and Peyton start pushing."

James stared down at the image of the dilapidated hospital, windows cracked and trash strewn outside. It made him think of the cops still in the hospital after their encounter with the Ghost, and he let out a low growl.

Time to clean up my mess.

Senator Johnston rested comfortably in his chair, a leather-bound copy of *A Tale of Two Cities* in hand. He had reread the book each year since he'd first read it as a boy. It always reminded him of both the suffering of the people when their leaders became indulgent and corrupt, and how that suffering could metastasize into something just as corrupt and terrible when left unaddressed. It was a lesson that any professional politician should keep in mind.

His secure phone chimed from atop a stand near his chair. He reached over and picked it up.

"Always some crisis. Let's see the damage today." The senator chuckled and looked at his text log. He frowned as he saw that the last one was from an unknown number.

FENRIR WAKES. LOOKS LIKE HE WANTS AN EAGLE FOR DINNER.

The senator let out a long sigh. "Damn, and I was having such a good day."

He brought up his contracts list and scrolled down until he arrived at "Aunt Matilda." He reached into his pocket and pulled out a portable DNA and retinal scanner, which he connected to his phone. He dialed the number.

Four melodic notes played when it answered.

"Johnston, Angus," he intoned. He placed his thumb on the silver pad and grimaced at the burn before placing his eye over the retinal scanner.

Four different melodic notes played.

It was time for the passphrase.

The senator inhaled deeply and quoted *Tom Sawyer*. "Tom said to himself that it was not such a hollow world, after all. He had discovered a great law of human action, without knowing it—namely, that in order to make a man or a boy covet a thing, it is only necessary to make the thing difficult to attain."

Wonder what Sam Clemens would think of our modern world? Same corruption, but now with magic. Talk about interesting times to be alive.

"Receipt of your call has been acknowledged and recorded," a man replied. "Please note that Protocol 2038 is now active per existing procedures, and will stay active until explicitly countermanded by the President."

"Duly noted, son." The senator took a deep breath. The next few days might amount to nothing more than rumors on the internet for the bulk of humanity, or they might change everything the same way Oriceran had, but if he and the rest of the government in the know about extraterrestrial life were doing their damned jobs, it'd be the former.

Never liked Project Ragnarok, Fortis, or any of the other bastards who were supposed to be protecting us. Asking a soldier to lay down his life in defense of his country and planet is one thing. At least he knows the deal. But what good is a government that sacrifices its citizens without asking because they aren't confident they can protect them?

Johnston snorted. Just call him Theseus. No more innocent sacrifices. He might not make all the calls, but for this first play, he was the quarterback.

"Pursuant to the protocol, I need alpha-class heavy strike teams with air support, both tactical and strategic level. I want coverage of about three hundred miles per team with rapid response capabilities, up to and including dedicated PDA support. Have them all on combat standby. Please pass up a potential Cleansing Fire solution to the

President with a recommendation of 'unnecessary at this time.' He'll have to be the one to authorize it."

The man on the other end audibly swallowed. "Yes, sir. Noted, sir."

Good, son. Always be afraid of nukes, even when they're ours.

"I also want dedicated 24/7 recon on James Brownstone. We need to know where he is at all times until Protocol 2038 is canceled."

"Yes, sir. Anything else?"

The senator frowned. "Nothing more. Say a few extra prayers over the next few days, son."

"Sir?"

"God helps those who help themselves." The senator ended the call and sighed.

CHAPTER EIGHTEEN

Trey yawned and patted his mouth with his hand. "Damn, is this shit boring! I've got a new respect for cops having to sit around on stake-outs and shit. We don't even have donuts and coffee."

Trey's F-350 sat in a crowded parking lot across from a busy bar. They were so close they didn't even need binoculars to see most people's faces through the side windows.

Victoria idly examined her nails, which were painted bright red. "Are you sure about being this close? We can see everything, but we're in a huge-ass truck, and everyone can see us. Someone might not like the fact that bounty hunters are sitting here watching a Mafia bar."

"Maybe they can't see us. We're not the ones sitting in a lit-up bar."

"They can probably see this big-ass truck."

"Big fucking deal. They can handle it. We've made it fucking clear around town that we're not interested in trash right now. Those fuckers just have to listen." Trey shrugged. "And they don't want to get in our way until we've snagged the Ghost. If I was these Mafia guys, maybe I'd be going to town and having a great time for the next few days or however long it takes us to find the Ghost."

"It's funny when you think about it." Victoria sighed. "The low-level guys are easy to track down because they don't have the muscle and resources to hide themselves, and the high-level guys are easy because they're usually too arrogant to completely hide, but this Silver Ghost is really doing a good job of keeping herself scarce. I wasn't certain about your false level five theory, but the more I think about it, the more it makes sense. If she's half as powerful as everyone keeps saying, she'd be pulling a Brownstone and issuing public challenges to criminals. I just wish she'd crawl up from the sewer already. And I agree with you— stake-outs are boring."

"Don't matter much. The entire Brownstone Agency is looking for the bitch, and the cops, too. If she pops up in LA or Vegas again, we're gonna nail her." Trey grinned. "I went ahead and told the other teams that if they spot her to let me know, but not to engage. They ain't you or me. They'll get fucked up if they try."

"You've been getting a lot of texts. No sightings?" Victoria frowned.

Trey shook his head. "Boring shit. Everyone's frustrated, because it's like the minute we stop chasing other bounties, those criminal bastards all start walking in front of us, almost like they're taunting us and shit, but we can't do anything because they're just the bait." He gestured at the bar. "Just like all those Mafia fucks inside are. From what I've heard, that particular family has been pushing themselves into some nasty shit. They sound like the kind of people who'd get a vigilante after them. It's why I picked this spot for us. Our best bet, assuming the Silver Ghost is even in town. According to some shit Heather passed along, her and Peyton did some computer shit, and their program says the Ghost might have a better chance of being in Vegas right now than LA, and will probably be going after the family we're watching. Who the fuck knows, though, right?"

"Speaking of family men, we might have some trouble." Victoria nodded toward the restaurant.

Two suited goons in too-tight suits stood in front of the doorway, gesturing in the general direction of the truck.

"Whatever. Fuckers." Trey reached into his pocket to slip on his gloves. "They best not be shooting up my baby, or I'm gonna go more Brownstone than Brownstone on them." He opened the door and stepped out. "You stay here. You don't have to listen to me, but you might not want to magic up yet. That might set them off."

Victoria grinned. "Let's see how good you are at talking your way out of this situation. Sometimes your mouth can be a weapon."

"That it is. That it is." Trey walked to the front of his truck and leaned against it, his arms crossed, staring at the two goons in open defiance. All negotiations should be started from a position of power, and in this case, he could back things up.

They frowned. One of the goons leaned in to say something to the other, who nodded. A few seconds later, they walked toward a crosswalk and waited for the walk signal.

Various cars zoomed by at high speed as the bounty

hunter and the mobsters continued to watch each other, neither side betraying emotion.

Trey looked around and sighed. Lincolns. Lexuses. BMWs. Mercedes. Too many damned fancy expensive cars.

Don't be starting shit, you dumb motherfuckers, especially in a parking lot. Only two of you fuckers. You won't have a chance anyway.

"Maybe these are all mob fuckers' cars," he murmured. "It might be funny to beat them up after all."

The walk signal popped on and the mobsters jogged across the street, slowing when they hit the new sidewalk so they could channel more swagger into their strut as they approached the bounty hunter.

Trey yawned again and lowered his arms but kept his hand out of his jacket. He wasn't afraid of the mobsters, but he didn't want to start an unnecessary fight and risk either his truck or the life of any innocent bastard who might be sitting in the mob-controlled bar.

It made him think of Johnny Lee. From what witnesses had passed on to the police, one of the man's last decent acts on Earth was to clear out everybody but his boys when he realized trouble was coming. No innocent people got caught in the crossfire.

Even gangsters have morals. Shit, what am I saying? I used to be a gang member. Maybe if James had gotten his hands on Johnny Lee and his boys, he could have turned them around too.

Trey clucked his tongue, thinking of one of Nana's favorite sayings. "There but for the grace of God go I."

The men closed to a few yards away, still on the sidewalk, a small chain running through cement posts the only thing separating them from the parking lot.

"Nice night," Trey announced, his voice full of cheer. "Don't you agree, gentlemen?" He inhaled. "Not too cold. Not too hot." He shrugged. "I'm sure as fine suit-wearers yourselves, you can appreciate the problem of being in a suit in Vegas in the middle of the day in May." He laughed. "That shit I'm gonna have to get used to. LA people like to think it's hot, but five degrees here and ten degrees there makes a huge difference. Oh, you should know before you say whatever it is you're about to say, that I'll be moving here all permanent-like soon. Keep that in mind. Don't want to get on my bad side."

The two goons exchanged frowns. Trey didn't recognize them, but that only meant they had no bounties and he hadn't kicked their asses before. The Brownstone Agency presence in Las Vegas might be spreading, but they still maintained a far lower profile than they did in Los Angeles and probably would for the near future, even with Trey there.

One of the goons cleared his throat. "You're Trey Garfield, right?"

Trey gave them his best smile, the one he normally reserved for his grandmother. "That's me, yes. Trey Garfield with the Brownstone Agency. At your service and all that shit." He offered them an exaggerated bow.

The goon frowned. "What are you doing here?" He nodded toward the bar. "You know who owns that place, right?"

"Yeah, I know who owns that place." Trey shrugged and glanced at Victoria, who was watching the confrontation unfold. The tip of her golden wand was barely visible above the dashboard, but the mobsters might not know what they were seeing if they looked that way.

"That's the problem, you see?" the goon replied. He flexed his fingers a few times, and his mouth twitched. "We can't have bounty hunters sitting outside family businesses. It's not good."

Trey snorted. "I ain't here for any of your family, so why do you care?"

"It makes us look bad to have a bounty hunter just sitting out here. It makes it look like we can't guarantee the safety of our customers. That makes us seem weak." The goon frowned, and his friend nodded in agreement.

"So, what, you think someone's gonna take a swing at you because little old Trey and his partner are sitting in a parking lot? Shit, not my fucking problem."

The goon's hand inched toward his jacket. The other man moved farther to the side, his hand also rising.

How many of you will I need to beat down for you to get the point?

"It's your problem because you're the cause of the problem," the goon growled. "If you get in your truck right now and leave, we don't need to have a problem. Sounds fair, don't you think?"

Trey snorted. "You dumb motherfucker. I ain't here for no Mafia shit, and ain't even here for no normal bounty shit. Haven't you fuckers been listening to me at all? Silver Ghost is out there."

The two men's hands dropped.

The first goon shook his head. "The Silver Ghost isn't real."

"Then who fucking killed the 25K Triad bitches? You

telling me some other gang or someone else did that shit but they didn't take credit?" Trey scoffed. "We both know that's not how this shit works for either bounty hunters or you bitches."

"E-even if she's real, she won't necessarily come after us. It's a big city."

Trey nodded. "Yeah, it is at that. LA's a much bigger city, and Johnny Lee and his boys are still dead, ain't they?" He scratched the side of his nose. "Here's the thing. Until the Silver Ghost is caught, Brownstone Agency is gonna be all over you fuckers because we want *her*, which means Brownstone Agency is basically giving the motherfucking Mafia free protection from a vigilante who could clear out this whole town."

"You just want the bounty," the goon insisted. "You want us to be grateful for that?"

"Bitch, please. Even if we do, you like living, right?" Trey gestured toward the bar. "Maybe that bitch won't come here at all. Maybe she never comes back to Vegas, but me and my people will stay out of your fucking way if you stay out of ours." He shrugged. "Or you can take us on and we'll beat you down, so then you'll be hurt, and you'll be wasting our time."

Trey stared down the two goons in silence. He wasn't sure how much time passed before they both turned and headed back to the crosswalk.

"Have a good evening, gentlemen," Trey called after them. "Remember, if you see the Ghost, call us. The life you save may be your own." He grinned. "And we'll give you a reward."

One of the goons flipped him off as they crossed the street.

Trey sauntered back over to his truck and hopped inside. "Not sure if that shit means I'm badass enough to scare fuckers off or if they're just afraid of the Ghost."

Victoria shrugged. "Don't see how it matters as long as they left us alone."

"True that." Trey sighed. "But now back to doing nothing but waiting."

His phone buzzed with a text, and he pulled it out of his coat pocket. A huge smile took over his face as he read the text.

Victoria arched a pale red brow. "What? Did you just get a text for a three-for-one deal on black suits and ties at the Men's Warehouse?"

"Nah. Just a lucky bastard today. My sleazy boy Anthony's just earned himself a payday. Silver Ghost sighting, and it's nearby."

"You think she's coming here?"

"Nah. According to Anthony, there's a Mafia safehouse a few miles away, and she's closer to that." Trey started his truck. "He did his part, now let's do ours."

CHAPTER NINETEEN

Trey grinned to himself as they barreled down the road. Considering they were going fifteen over the limit, a cop could have pulled them over, but no one came after them. Sure, some traffic drone was probably tagging his license plate and he'd get a fine in the mail in a couple of weeks, but for the moment, all he cared about was getting to the safehouse before the Silver Ghost escaped.

We'll end this shit, and then we can all go back to making money and taking down crooks.

He slammed on the brakes, the truck screeching to a halt in front of an unassuming ranch-style house with a verdant and carefully trimmed lawn. The illusion of order was broken by the spider-webbed cracks marring some of the windows, and the front door stood open.

Trey frowned and nodded to Victoria. "You ready for this?"

The witch nodded, her suit already covered with protective glyphs and her eyes glowing red. "If she doesn't immediately surrender, we'll need to go at her full force. Hit hard and fast until she's dead."

"Yeah, I know." Trey pulled out his gun and ejected the magazine. He loaded his single magazine of anti-magic bullets. "This bitch is going down."

Both bounty hunters exited the truck at the same time. Trey took point, his gun raised, Victoria trailing behind him, her wand at the ready.

A few yards of walking toward the front porch revealed two dead men in the living room, one with a huge gash across his chest, the other a charred hole in his back.

"If she's not here, at least she's been here," Trey murmured. "She ain't subtle, that's for sure."

"What misfortune you have," came a voice from above. "That you would arrive before I left. More parasites, flocking to your deaths."

Trey jerked his gun up. The Silver Ghost stood on the roof, moonlight highlighting her metallic form. Blood dripped from an arm blade and splattered all over her as if she'd been decorated by a homicidal Jackson Pollock.

Damn. I wonder if this is what bounties feel like when the big man shows up?

The Silver Ghost tilted her head, as smooth and featureless as ever. "Not what I was expecting. Not more Mafia. I know you, Trey Garfield." She glanced at the witch. "And you, Victoria Stone."

Trey grinned. "Good, that makes this shit easy. We ain't no Mafia bitches. We're with the Brownstone Agency. Silver Ghost, or whatever name you like, there is a level-five bounty on you placed by the City and County of Los Angeles. You need to surrender right now, and we'll have the Vegas police secure you. Then I'm sure Vegas and LA can fight over who wants you. This shit don't have to be rough."

The Silver Ghost let out a soft chuckle. "You expect me to surrender to you, of all people?"

"It'd be nice, yeah." Trey shrugged. "I know you've been kicking a lot of ass, but you ain't faced no one like Victoria and me. I've got anti-magic bullets and magical artifacts. She's a badass battle witch. This won't be about cutting up surprised mobsters and bouncing regular bullets off."

"Haven't you heard? The AET used anti-magic bullets, and it didn't help them."

Victoria narrowed her eyes, her fingers tightening on her wand.

Trey nodded. "Then I'll waste a lot of money, but I'm sure the big man won't mind. If the bullets don't work, between Vic and me, we've got plenty of ways to mess your shit up. Look, I know how it feels. Some of these pieces of shit I've run into, I've thought, 'Yeah, why do we have to wait for a bounty?' But we can't have that shit. You do things right, proper, and thorough, and things can start getting cleaned up. LA and Vegas might not be perfect, but we're making progress. You can't just be slicing people's heads off."

"I don't care what you have to say," the Silver Ghost replied. Her blade flowed back into a normal arm and hand.

She says she don't care, but she's disarming. This shit's working. Yeah, time for Smooth Trey.

"Look, you pissed off the big man when you hurt those cops." Trey shrugged. "But you didn't waste them even though you could have, so I'm trying to give you a chance. I think you've kind of gone too far, but I get that you probably have a good reason for doing your vigilante shit. That don't mean I can let you go, though. We just don't have to have trouble.

The Silver Ghost chuckled. "The big man is James Brownstone, correct?"

"Yeah. Not an official nickname or anything, just what I call him. Granite Ghost. Scourge of Harriken."

"The monster who hunts monsters." The Silver Ghost crouched. "It doesn't make sense. It's been too long, but I can't be wrong. I've seen him use it."

"Huh?"

"He's a monster. You can't see it?"

Trey laughed. "You're running around chopping people's heads off without bounties, and you're saying *he's* the monster? Come on, girl, think about that."

He wondered if he should lower his weapon, but even with Victoria covering him, that felt unwise. His tight gut and pounding heart told him talking it out might not work.

"Denounce James Brownstone," the Silver Ghost demanded, "and I'll spare your lives."

Trey's face scrunched in confusion. "What?"

The Silver Ghost sliced through the air with her palm. "Denounce him. He's a monster." Her head twitched a few times. "You're not like this woman. I can tell. You've been deceived."

What the fuck is wrong with her?

Trey chanced a glance at Victoria, but the witch was keeping her gaze locked on their opponent.

The Silver Ghost's skin rippled like water, and she

hissed, "I've been forced to become a monster to deal with him. When my people come, they'll hate me for what I've done. Curse my name and claim I've made a mockery of what I swore to be. Despite all that, when I ask myself if I should tell you the truth, I find myself bound to my oaths. It's pathetic. What oaths does James Brownstone honor other than plotting murder and death?" Her skin rippled again, and her head twitched.

"Look…" Trey sucked in a deep breath. Calling her names wouldn't help. "I don't know what your problem with James is. He can get heavy, but that's only when people come at him. You see, that's the difference." He shook his head. "I used to be a street thug, and your ass would have cut me down like nothing, but James saw something and lifted me up. You think you're cleaning up LA and Vegas? James Brownstone is doing that. Carrot and stick, not just a sharpened stick, you know what I'm saying?"

"Yes, I know all about your background, Trey Garfield. All about the background of your little parasites." The Silver Ghost stood and marched toward the edge of the roof. "Is that the connection? Does Brownstone see you as expendable?" She shook her head. "I don't understand him. I know what he is. He's not behaving as he should, but he's still violent and bloodthirsty."

Trey cleared his throat. "You know, this may start some shit, but have you ever thought you're just a little crazy, and maybe that's making it hard for you to understand?"

Victoria glared at him, and he shrugged. He was tired of this murderous vigilante running down James. She was the one with a bounty, not him.

"Crazy?" The Silver Ghost leapt into the air.

Trey didn't fire, only because her trajectory took her away from him. She landed with ease, no hint of strain from jumping twenty feet to the ground.

Victoria took a few steps back, her fingers so tight around her wand that she might have cut off her circulation.

The Silver Ghost's head swiveled back and forth. It was hard to tell without a face, but presumably, she was looking at the two bounty hunters.

So, she hasn't got 360 vision or some shit like that. That's good to know.

"It's taking too long to calibrate," she explained. "The instability is making it increasingly harder to concentrate. I've waited too long." She sighed. "I should have gone after him earlier."

"What the fuck does any of that mean?"

"In a sense, you're right. You could say I'm getting increasingly crazy." The Silver Ghost shrugged. "It doesn't matter. A sacrifice had to be made to save everyone. What happens to me isn't important, so I'll give you this one last chance, Trey Garfield and Victoria Stone. Denounce James Brownstone, lower your weapons, and I'll consider letting you live."

"Fuck you," Trey shouted.

Victoria cleared her throat. "I'm not going to claim that I believe in Brownstone as much as Trey, but from what I've seen, he's the horse I want to back. You just got done explaining how even *you* know you're a nutjob."

"I'm running out of time," the Silver Ghost replied. "It's unfortunate, but you leave me no choice, and your threats suggest you'll be useful for more testing and calibration. I'll even let you have the first shot."

Trey's finger twitched on his trigger. "I ain't here to kill you. Just stand down."

"Ah, so you do have some restraint. It was wise of me not to cut you down without reason, but let me make something very clear. I won't surrender to you." The Silver Ghost took a step forward. "I was going to leave you alive because I've looked into your backgrounds and found that although both of you were formerly parasites, you have shown improvement—other than working for that monster—but now I need more calibration, and you'll provide it. If you won't denounce him, you'll atone for your service in another way."

"Stop moving," Trey demanded. "Put your hands on your head, and if you can shut down your armor or whatever, do it."

The Silver Ghost raised her right arm, which rippled and flowed into a sharp blade. "Goodbye, Trey Garfield."

Three quick trigger pulls from Trey followed. The Silver Ghost stumbled back, three new small indents in her head, but no blood. The crushed bullets fell to the ground a few seconds later.

"Damn it," Victoria muttered. Golden energy blasted from her wand and struck their enemy's side.

The Silver Ghost's skin rippled around the wound, and she stumbled. There was a gaping hole, but no sign of blood or any sort of internal structure other than more smooth silver material.

What the fuck is she?

Trey kept firing, but it felt like he was inconveniencing

the Ghost rather than hurting her, and that was annoying considering how many expensive bullets he was putting into her.

Will you die already?

Victoria followed up with another attack, this time blasting a hole in the Silver Ghost's head. The vigilante stumbled and fell to one knee.

With a click, Trey's gun signaled it was empty. He slapped in a new magazine filled with conventional rounds and shook his head. "This shit didn't have to go down like that."

His witch partner didn't say anything, instead firing a third shot through the Silver's Ghost chest. The wounded vigilante fell backward.

Victoria let out a sigh of relief. "I put in a little more energy into those than normal, so they weren't as fast as I would have liked, but it looks like it was worth it."

Trey snorted. "Told you she weren't all that. I also admit that if you weren't here, I might have had some trouble." He grinned. "Don't let it go to your head."

"It's strange."

It took Trey a few seconds to realize it wasn't Victoria talking. He jerked his head back toward the Silver Ghost.

The woman sat up, the holes and dents in her body sealing. "Redundancy and distribution of what passes for my mind. If all these pieces of me are me, what am I? I wonder if that's part of the reason I'm losing control. I don't have a soul anymore. A normal body isn't supposed to function like this, but it does make me realize I'm stronger than even Brownstone. I doubt he could survive this."

Trey opened fire, but the bullets didn't penetrate any better than before.

Victoria fired another blast, but this time the attack didn't cut a hole through the enemy.

The Silver Ghost stalked forward. "Not perfect, not like that monster, but almost as effective. Additional testing and calibration. It was worth the loss of material."

Trey threw his gun on the ground and raised his fists. He charged the Ghost and threw a punch. His fist smacked into her head, and it jerked back, revealing a slight indent. She slammed her non-blade arm into him, and he flew backward with a grunt, pain spiking through his chest.

He crashed into a wall and fell face-first onto the lawn, leaving a shallow dent in the wall. A few ribs ached, but he'd felt worse.

Heart pounding, Trey hopped to his feet. He shook his head just in time to see the Silver Ghost stab at Victoria. The blade hit, and a bright flash blinded him. When his vision cleared, he noticed that the glyphs on her suit had dimmed considerably.

The vigilante stepped back, the tip of her blade now missing. "Impressive. That cost me more material than I wanted to use." She leapt backward, landing twenty feet away.

Victoria grinned. "Can't kill me if you can't hit me. Guess we win after all."

The Silver Ghost threw up both her arms. Golden energy circled both and fused together before shooting toward the witch.

The attack struck Victoria in the stomach and she cried out, falling backward. The glyphs on her suit vanished, and a deep, charred wound covered her stomach. She raised her wand, her arm shaking.

Her enemy rushed toward her as the witch fired again. The attack narrowly missed.

The Silver Ghost kicked the wand out of her hand and stomped on her fingers. Victoria hissed in pain.

"I ain't down yet!" Trey shouted, and charged.

The Silver Ghost whipped her arm up and fired a blast straight into his leg. Agony exploded from his wounded limb to the rest of his body, and he tumbled to the ground, his vision swimming and his heart doing its best to force its way out of his chest.

"Excellent," the Silver Ghost declared. "Despite a few missteps, this proves how effective my calibration has been. I'll admit you put up a better fight than most I've tested myself against. A few other things will need to be adjusted before I deal with Brownstone, but I'm much more confident than I was before."

Victoria crawled toward her wand. The Silver Ghost impaled her leg, and the witch screamed. Her eyes rolled up and she passed out, but her chest still rose and fell.

Damn it. I got to get a healing potion into her.

The silver-skinned vigilante yanked her blade out of Victoria and sauntered toward Trey, her blade up. "Denounce James Brownstone, or you will die here, Trey Garfield."

"Fuck you. James saved my life and made me a better man. Even if I die here, at least I'm not dying on the street fighting some other bitch for territory. I'm not gonna go out like a pussy. I'd sooner die than say anything bad about James." Trey tried to focus on the woman heading toward him. If he lost consciousness, it'd be all over. He could still maybe get a punch in.

"Denounce James Brownstone." The Silver Ghost brought her blade to his neck. "Your defenses have obviously been exceeded. You won't survive my next attack."

Trey spat on the blade. He didn't have the angle or strength to get it to her face.

"Do it, bitch. Trey Garfield ain't going out on anyone's terms but his own. Don't matter what happens to me. James will find you and kill you, and your psycho crusade will be over."

The blade advanced until it drew a drop of blood. "You enjoy being a parasite of a different sort, hurting people. That's all this is. Your improvement is a lie. Tell me I'm wrong."

"Fuck you. I wouldn't mind if every bounty surrendered without any trouble." Trey ground his teeth over the throbbing in his leg. "You're the one who thinks she's judge, jury, and executioner. Even those 25K or the Mafia bitches in this house—you can't say they've done shit to you. At least when the big man took down the Harriken, it was because they'd hurt his dog and kept coming after him."

The Silver Ghost inched her weapon away from his neck. "I'm not wrong. You don't understand. It's impossible for his kind to be anything other than what they are." Her voice pitched up. "I'm not wrong!" she screamed and raised the blade over her head.

Trey closed his eyes.

I'm coming, Shorty. I'm sorry, brother. I got cocky. I can't even say I'm going out a hero like you did.

He waited for the blow. After ten seconds, he opened his eyes.

"Why?" The Silver Ghost shook her head and dropped her blade to her side. "It's not...possible." Her blade flowed back into her arm, and she clutched her head. "You don't understand. None of you. You're being tricked. Deceived. It doesn't matter what he's like now. He'll turn on you. Kill you all." Her head twitched a few times. "Everything I've done, I've done to protect people. Everything I've done, I've done to protect this planet." She backed up several steps, shaking her head. "Don't you understand? I've given up my very soul. The Spirits won't receive me now that I've become this...thing, but I did it all for you." She laughed. "It doesn't matter. I'll destroy Brownstone soon, and then you'll see. You'll all see."

She turned and leapt onto a neighbor's roof, then bounded away, house by house.

Trey groaned and reached into his pocket to grab a healing potion. He downed it and waited for the long seconds to pass as his pain faded and his wounds closed.

After a few deep breaths, he rushed over to Victoria and fished a potion out of her pocket and forced the contents down her throat. Once her wounds had disappeared, he grabbed an energy potion from another of his pockets and emptied it down her throat.

A few seconds later, Victoria's eyes fluttered open, and she sat up, coughing.

Trey let out a sigh of relief. "You okay, Vic?"

"That was fucking embarrassing. I don't think I've ever had my ass handed to me so badly." The witch pinched the bridge of her nose. "What happened? Did you get her?" She looked around the yard for the other woman.

Trey shook his head. "She left. Threatened the big man and left after another big rant."

Sirens sounded in the distance.

Victoria crawled over to grab her wand, then stood to brush the grass and dirt off her pants. "No, Trey, turns out we're not ready for level fives. Even ones by themselves."

Trey managed a chuckle. "Yeah, I kind of noticed. I'll call the big man and let him know what happened. Don't worry. If we got close, so can he."

CHAPTER TWENTY

Thomas barked as James stomped back and forth in his living room, his hands fisted. It was hard to tell who had growled more over the last few minutes, the man or the dog.

"I'm fucking tired of this Silver Ghost. I need to end this shit. Trey and Victoria could have been killed," James thundered. "And I'm not losing more people."

Shay sighed from the couch. "It's okay, James. They both survived. I'm sure Trey learned his lesson. I get why he thought what he thought. It's not like I've never misjudged a threat, and the important thing is, he and Victoria are still breathing."

"Fuck that. I'm not mad about that." James shook his head. "Sometimes a man has to push himself. I get that. I wish he hadn't been a dumbass, but it doesn't matter. He doesn't know who and what she really is. Maybe if he did, he wouldn't have gone after her. That's the problem. This bitch wants a Vax Forerunner, and I want to meet her and show her what a Vax Forerunner can do."

"'Sometimes a man has to push himself?'" Shay raised an eyebrow. "Figures you'd say something like that. I should have known, but anyway, we need to focus on what we can learn from what happened."

James stopped his angry stomping and crossed his arms. "But if Trey passed along what she said right, then she did something to herself. It almost sounds like she can adapt like Whispy."

Shay frowned. "Yeah, they blew a hole in her head, yet somehow she didn't die. We know she has those nanites. I'm no expert on alien technology, but I'm thinking maybe she did something like you did. You've told me how Whispy has talked about modifying you several times. What if she used those nanites to do the same thing? But who knows? Maybe she found some crazy gnome to enchant her or something. I don't think the how is as important as the what."

"Yeah. We know she can regenerate and partially adapt to attacks. She's an energy weapon who can beat powerful magical shields. That Wendigo nanoform seemed like it could do some of the same things, but I just needed to get a few hits in with Whispy to win. If she's that dependent on nanites, it'll be a short fight."

"Don't make the same mistake Trey did."

James grunted. "What the fuck are you talking about? I'm not Trey. I've got Whispy."

"You heard him when he talked about her. He assumed a lot of things because of what happened before, but she was a lot more powerful than he expected. He was going into a fight he expected to win, not a curb-stomp. If she's ready to take you on and knows what you are, that means she has some hope of beating you. That's all I'm saying." Shay shrugged. "A lot of people get cocky and want to take you on, but this woman's been avoiding you. Now it sounds like she's ready to stop that."

"I don't give a fuck," James growled. "She's fucked with you, me, my city, the cops, and now my people. You've tried to talk to her, and Trey talked to her. It doesn't matter. I'm through worrying about anything but taking this bitch down. I don't care what her reasons are. If she has a problem with the Vax, she can take it up with them. She's had too many chances. This shit ends, especially since if what Trey says is right and she's fucking losing it. It's only a matter of time until she goes and blows up a stadium or some shit to get me. She needs to die, and fast."

"Hey, I'm on your side." Shay held up her hands. "I've wanted to kill the bitch for a long time. I'm just worried it won't be as easy as we hoped, even with Whispy, and I want you to keep that in mind and be careful."

James stomped over to his chair and dropped into it so hard it almost tipped over. Thomas barked and rushed over to lay down next to the chair, tail wagging.

"We stick to the plan," James rumbled. "Heather and Peyton are doing what they can to bait her to the hospital. I'll finish her off there once and for all, and this shit will be over."

Shay nodded. "What if she doesn't come tomorrow?"

"Then I'll fucking issue a public challenge. I'm sure if I go to the news they'll eat that shit up. Then I can pick the Salton Sea or something. It's riskier, but I'll do what I need to do to end this shit." James gritted his teeth.

If only he had blood or hair or something, they could at

least try to track her. The police told him the PDA was trying to track her and not coming up with anything, but he wasn't sure if that meant she had a special technique to block magic or their options were limited in similar ways to his.

"There's another possibility we might consider." Shay licked her lips, her eyes darting to the side. "Even though I'm not crazy about it."

"What?"

Shay took a deep breath and let it out. "We call the government and tell them what is happening. Either via the Professor and Correk, or maybe Senator Johnston."

James frowned. "I thought you were the one who was worried about them coming after me."

"I still am, but they have entire projects devoted to preparing for aliens. They might have a few special guns or something." Shay shrugged. "Doesn't hurt to have backup."

"No. Fuck that." James let out a dark chuckle. "I'm a fucking Vax Forerunner, right? Some badass alien super-soldier. There's nothing the government's going to bring to the table that I won't be able to do if I'm pissed enough, and I'm really, really pissed right now."

Shay nodded. "Then we stick to the plan. Given what happened to Trey, I doubt any more of your people will try to get close to her. Let's hope we can point her at that hospital for tomorrow night."

James had just slipped underneath the covers when his phone rang. He rolled over to pick it up. Unknown number.

He snatched up the phone and yawned. "Who is this?"

"Tell me one thing, Vax. When is the invasion?"

James growled. "It's you, bitch. What should I call you, Erin or the Silver Ghost?"

"I've come to enjoy the name 'Silver Ghost.' It doesn't matter. The being I was before is effectively gone, but it's worth it to have become a weapon to fight you."

"You won't fucking listen. I'm not what you think."

"A Forerunner? I know you are. I've seen it several times." The Silver Ghost chuckled. "It is...interesting to see how you've chosen to wield your power, and it confuses me. I've thought about it for a long time. There's still so much the Nine Systems Alliance doesn't know about the symbiont-host relationship. The few we've managed to capture don't last that long. When it becomes obvious you can't escape, the symbionts end it, from what we can tell. Convenient that, but it occurs to me that an invasion at this point would be futile. Some Oriceran would just open a portal, and they'd kick you into the World in Between. Can your technology get you out of that, murderer?"

James growled. "You've hurt a lot of people who didn't have it coming. I don't want to hear shit from you about anything."

Shay bolted upright and grabbed her own phone. She started furiously tapping.

"This ends very soon, Vax," the Silver Ghost replied. "You will die. Don't even bother with threats about your glorious power. I have no intention of surviving this battle. It will be sufficient that I take you with me."

James grunted. "Fine, then maybe we should pick a place where no one will get hurt. You're the refugee queen and all that shit. You should care more than I do. How about the Salton Sea?"

The Silver Ghost snorted. "No. Here's my theory, Brownstone. I think your symbiont is letting you think for yourself until it gets all the information and adaptations it needs, and then it'll take over. A different strategy for a unique situation. Two linked planets. Still, it's pathetic in a way. You're as much a victim as anyone, but that doesn't change the fact that you're a clear and present danger to the planet, and I will kill you."

"Fuck you. You can't win. You're so fucking afraid of me that you've done everything you can not to come at me directly. In that armor, I'm invincible, and you know it." James snorted. "That's why you refuse to come to the Salton Sea, you fucking coward."

"Do you think you can goad me so easily, Vax?" The Silver Ghost sighed. "I've looked thoroughly into your human persona. There are many obvious holes in it, with your obvious lack of empathy and simple understanding. You're a shell, a monster who has learned to fake human emotions. You know why? Because you were nothing to begin with. You're just supposed to be a body for your symbiont. But I learned my lesson, and now we can fight on even terms."

"Then fight me already!" James yelled.

Thomas rushed into the room and started barking.

Shay continued tapping at her phone, occasionally reading a text sent to her.

"Oh, we'll fight soon, but this isn't about honor or ego, Vax. Once your symbiont takes over, all it cares about is victory. I'm not going to give you the chance. I haven't gone after you directly thus far because all my information suggests your neighbors are innocents, so I'll wait. Maybe I'll wait until you're distracted." A mocking laugh followed. "If you really want me to come, go hunt more bounties. I'm going to do whatever it takes to gain the advantage over you. I've sacrificed my life and very soul to defeat you. Sentry 7921, Shepherd 2nd Class Aiyn Noraz Hal died. I'm the spirit of her vengeance, lingering in this world to finish you off. So wait and wonder, Vax. And know fear."

She hung up.

James dropped his phone before he crushed it by accident. "The bitch wouldn't bite." He glanced at Shay. "You talking to Peyton?"

Shay nodded. "Was trying to get him to trace the call, but you weren't on long enough."

Thomas hopped on the bed and barked.

James scratched behind his ears. "Sorry, boy. Just some bitch bothering me." He turned to Shay. "She said something about how she was going to hit me when I least expected it. Even said I should go after bounties."

Shay looked down at her phone and quickly typed in a message. "That's good."

"Good? How the fuck is that good? I can't kill her if she won't come at me."

"As far as the underworld's concerned, you're going after a bounty soon who is hiding out in that hospital.

From what you told me, Maria's made sure the cops know the truth, so the only risk we have is other bounty hunters or criminals showing up." Shay shrugged. "Not optimal, but it'll be minimal risk of innocent people, anyway."

"You're saying she's ready to take the bait?"

"Yeah, I think she is. She leaked too much information to Trey. Whether it's alien steroids, nanites, or something else, whatever she did is messing with her and she's running out of time. She can't wait." A thoughtful look passed over Shay's face. "I'm sure she'll come at you there, so sure that maybe we should consider a trap. Get a few people, set some bombs—that sort of thing."

"No. No one else. The AET, Trey, and Victoria all got their asses handed to them. It's too risky, and I'm not afraid of her. No bullshit. If we try and set traps, she might run." James curled his hands into fists. "No, it's got to be clean to make her think she has the advantage. Heather and Peyton have been saying I'm going to show up around sunset, so she might show up earlier, but probably not too early, for the same reasons. If she doesn't show up, we'll figure out something else, but otherwise, I figure the best thing to do is drive over there tomorrow and scream until she shows up, then kill her."

"I'll go to Warehouse Three and grab my gear. I don't have a nice symbiont."

"No. I don't want you getting involved."

Shay glared at him. "What?"

"This bitch is obsessed with me, and I can win. Even if I don't win, once I'm dead, she'll either leave or die eventually." James reached out and stroked Shay's cheek. "You always bitch about me being stubborn. Some shit is just too much, even for you. I want you to promise me that no matter what, you'll stay out of it."

Shay groaned and averted her eyes. "Damn it, James. You want me to sit there and do nothing while some alien bitch is trying to kill my man?"

"Yeah, because your man is going to kill her first." A determined look swept James' face. "Promise me."

"Fine." Shay crossed her arms. "I won't go in with you, because you'll probably just do that paralysis bullshit again like you did the first time we tangled with the Council." She punched him in the arm. "And don't think I've forgotten that."

James grunted. "Be pissed all you want. I don't care as long as you're safe. Tomorrow night, I'll make it simple for both of us. Her name isn't Erin, by the way. It's Aiyn Noraz Hal."

Shay snorted. "Rest in fucking peace soon then, Aiyn Noraz Hal."

CHAPTER TWENTY-ONE

James took in the setting sun in the distance, the tall LA skyscrapers hiding it on occasion as the F-350 rumbled down the road. He'd spent a lot of time that day thinking about whether he should call Alison and let her know what was going on, but decided against it. She didn't need to worry, and he was going to win. What good would it do for her to know?

Shay sat in the passenger seat, frowning out the window, her hands in her lap.

I'm sorry, Shay. I know you're pissed, but there are some assholes only I can take on. I need to be focused now, and knowing you're safe means I'll be able to take down this alien.

The whole thing kicked his heart rate up in anger every time he thought about it. The Harriken might have been dicks, but at least he'd done something to them first. It wasn't like they were hunting him because his dad had killed a Harriken once.

The Vax probably did something to Aiyn's people. Maybe her family. Wiped them out, I'm guessing, but it doesn't matter. I'm not loyal to them, and she's lost it. This shit ends tonight, one way or another.

"How does it feel?" Shay asked, still staring out the window.

"How does what feel?"

She turned to look at him. "Knowing. You spent so many years not knowing what happened to your parents or what the amulet is, and now you know everything. I know what you told me, but that was before you were going to face down some obsessed alien who sees you as nothing but evil. I just wanted to make sure since you're benching me—which I'm gonna remind you about for years by the way—that you're going into this fight in the right headspace, not some brooding shit where you secretly think she's right about you being evil."

James pondered the idea. "Doesn't change anything. I feel the same way I did before. My parents sacrificed their lives for me. So did Father Thomas. I'm not gonna waste the life they gave me to make Aiyn Noraz Hal feel better about herself. I don't give a shit about the Vax, so I'm not gonna let her lay that on me."

"So you're not gonna let her mindfuck you?" Shay raised an eyebrow, a questioning look on her face.

"No fucking way. She's screwed with us for far too long. The only reason she got away with it was that we couldn't find her, and now she's saving us the trouble." James' hand tightened on the wheel. "I don't know about this Nine Systems Alliance, and I don't give a shit. It's not my responsibility to even keep every fucker on Earth in check, let alone Oriceran, and I don't even know where this Nine Systems Alliance is." He gritted his teeth. "You know what's not fucking simple? Bullshit about other planets. I try to stay away from Oriceran for the same reason, and now these aliens are bringing their fucking baggage to me on Earth."

Shay smiled. "Good. I'm glad to hear it, but if you *do* end up getting yourself killed, I'm gonna find some way to chase you into the afterlife and kill you again for being so stupid."

"How does that shit work? What happens if you kill me in the afterlife?"

"I don't know. You probably end in Laramie after that." She shrugged.

James chuckled.

"Hey, can you still hear me?" Heather sent over James' earpiece. Not going in with Shay didn't mean not taking advantage of other available assets.

Shay perked up. She also had an earpiece and could hear the conversation.

"Yeah, I can hear you," James replied. "What's up?"

"Two minutes ago, all our drone feeds from the area cut out. Peyton got a satellite image of the area, and there are some weird lighting artifacts. I can't connect to any cameras in the area, either."

"So she's there," James rumbled. "The bait worked."

Shay's expression darkened.

"That's what we figure," Heather offered. "Trying to send a few drones through again. We do know it's not an EMP. One of our drone feeds came back a minute after we lost it, but the drone was on a course away from the hospital."

James smiled. "Good. I was worried she might not show

up. You guys did a good job of luring her out here. This shit might have dragged on a long time without you, especially since she let months go by before she tried shit."

"Thanks, James, that means a lot, but you need to realize this also means we can't give you any active support. To be clear, whatever she's doing this time isn't just jamming signals. She's somehow blocking our ability to see into the interference zone from outside. It's not like it's dark or something, it's more like active camera spoofing. I don't even know how she's doing it since the drones haven't been compromised, so I can't even begin to set up a defense."

"Doesn't matter. I won't need help. Whatever happens tonight, this shit isn't gonna be hide and seek. She wants me dead, and that means she's gonna come at me." James slowed his truck. "How far out is the interference zone?"

"A few hundred yards from the hospital."

"I'm gonna park before that." James looked around. "I want Shay to stay in contact with you."

The neighborhood was rundown, with many boarded-up shops and condemned buildings. A few gang members lingered on the corners, conversing with prostitutes who didn't look like they were scoring many high-quality customers.

James wasn't worried about his truck. Shay would be there to keep people away from it, but avoiding parking his shiny well-maintained truck on the street wouldn't be the worst idea. Not planning on dying meant he would need his F-350 when the battle was over.

James spotted an alley sandwiched between an empty barbershop for rent and a closed Mongolian grill. The thought of grilled meat summoned a rather unexpected thought into his head.

Huh. After this shit is over, we should make a Jessie Rae's run. I'll deserve it.

James turned the truck into the alley and looked at Shay. "You're not gonna sneak out after me or some shit, are you?"

Shay rolled her eyes. "I promised, so I'll let you and Whispy do your thing. But if that bitch kills you, I'm not promising I'm letting her leave even if it gets me killed. I'll track her to whatever planet she slinks off to and kill her slowly and fucking painfully. She thinks the Vax are scary? Welcome to dealing with Shay Carson."

"Good to know." James shifted the car into Park and looked around. No one in the alley, a promising beginning to a not-so-fun-filled evening of ass-kicking.

Shay loaded a magazine into her gun from a box in the back. "Peyton, you've been quiet. You there?"

"Yes, I'm here," he replied through the earpiece. "I was just running some filtering algorithms to see if I can get through her weird area cloaking or spoofing or whatever the hell it is. It's pissing me off."

"Fine. Let me know the minute any of that drops."

James stared at her. "So you can charge in because you think I'm dead?"

"Yeah, basically. Understood, Peyton? I'd like Heather to do it, but I can't threaten to kill someone with a kid."

Heather snickered.

Peyton groaned. "You don't have to threaten me to get me to do it, you know."

"It's just a joke, though a little extra motivation never

hurt anyone," Shay replied. "James, I know it's a huge long-shot, but maybe because you'll be talking to her face to face, she'll buy a clue. She's coming after you at this hospital because she's worried about casualties, so no matter how nuts she is, maybe she's still reachable."

James reached underneath his shirt toward his amulet and rested his hand on the metal spacer. "Don't fucking care at this point. She hurt Trey, Victoria, and the cops. She needs to go down."

"Just saying, if you can get her to stall for a while, like a few weeks or a month, she might not last. She said she was on borrowed time."

"Doesn't matter, because she's not gonna last the next hour." James pulled his hand out of his shirt. No, not yet. It wasn't time, but the amulet reminded him he wanted to ensure Shay was well-protected in case a horde of gang members bum-rushed his truck.

He refused to hand over the engagement ring. There was no fucking way he was going to propose to her right before a fight. That didn't seem epic; it felt like pure desperation. It was the shit he saw in movies where some guy pulled out a picture of "his girl" right before he did a landing on a D-Day beach and got his head blown off. Best not to tempt fate.

James pulled the companion jade pendant out of his pocket and held it out in his hand. "It's a shield pendant—something I got from the Professor. Better than your rings. I guarantee it."

Shay slowly picked it up, a frown growing on her face. "When did you get this?"

"A while back. Just kind of wasn't ever the right time to

give it to you. Shit kept coming up." James picked up his phone and scrolled through his messages until he found the phonetic pronunciation and samples for the Old Mandarin activation passphrase. He forwarded the message to Shay.

He considered explaining about how it needed moonlight to fully recharge but telling her that right now felt like tempting fate again.

Not gonna make her sit here while I'm fighting a battle she can't see after making her think I'm marching off to die. Not fair to her, even though I'm going to kick Aiyn's ass back to space.

Shay slipped the pendant over her neck and leaned toward James to give him a deep kiss. She smiled softly as she pulled away. "Just remember, James, the only woman allowed to kill you is me."

"I'll keep that in mind. But don't worry, I'll be back soon. She won't." James threw open the door and hopped to the ground, then slammed the door and reached under his shirt.

It was time to become the bogeyman Aiyn feared so much.

James yanked the spacer off. Familiar pain shot through his chest as the amulet spread its technorganic tendrils through him.

Initiation, Whispy sent. Waves of excitement radiated from the amulet.

So you know what we're about to do?

Kill strong enemy. High adaptation potential.

Yeah, that's the long and short of it.

James jogged out of the alley and down the street

toward the hospital. He could just make out the gray outline of the five-story building in the distance.

A few gang members emerged from a dilapidated apartment building.

"So that's when I said, 'Yeah, bitch, that's my gun. What are you gonna fucking do about it'?" one of the gang members explained.

The others all laughed and looked at James, curious smirks on their faces. Their eyes widened.

"Oh, fuck. Is that James Brownstone? Which of you dumbass bitches got a bounty?"

The gang members scrambled back into the apartment building.

Not today, assholes. Don't have the time, and don't give a fuck. Even our new hires could beat your asses.

Relief spread over the men's faces when James continued past the apartment building.

"We're still trying to see if we can break through her interference somehow," Heather reported. "You sure about this, James? It's not too late to come up with a different plan."

"Damn fucking sure."

"Uh, I've got you on drone. You're not even wearing your coat, and I don't see a gun or any knives on you."

James grunted. "Don't need them. This isn't the kind of fight I'm going to win using that kind of gear, and no reason to waste a coat. She'd just shred it anyway. Even if I buy them in bulk, it's still wasting money."

"And you're sure about not calling AET? Or I don't know, the National Guard?"

"Yeah." James slowed. He'd likely be hitting the interference zone soon. "Gotta admit, when we finally told you the truth, I didn't know how you'd react. I half-wondered if you'd be freaked."

"In a world with elves, how weird are aliens, really? You make more sense to me in a lot of ways than crap like the Eyes."

"I'm weird enough." James grunted. "But you don't give a shit about any of this Vax Forerunner stuff? The truth is, from what I remember and what Aiyn said, I'm a living WMD when I'm paired with Whispy."

"So are a lot of Oricerans." Heather let out a quiet sigh. "Look, James, if you were going to turn evil, I think you would have done it a long time ago. I don't know anything about how things work outside of Earth and Oriceran, but both planets have plenty of races that tend toward pissing people off, but still have plenty of individuals who aren't total flaming dicks. You helped give me my life back, James. The least I can do is believe in you in return."

"Thanks, Heather."

"No pro—"

James frowned. "Heather?"

There was no response.

James looked over his shoulder. The shimmer in the air was slight. If he hadn't been specifically looking for something like it, he wasn't sure he would have noticed.

Whispy's excitement intensified.

Amulet aside, the next few minutes passed with no encounters.

Not a single person even close to the hospital? I doubt they're that scared of ghosts.

That made him wonder if Aiyn had some way of forcing people out of an area with her technology.

Whispy, can you tell if there is any sort of mental field being projected?

No significant link errors detected.

That would have to do.

James squinted. The continuing retreat of the sun made it hard to make out details on the hospital grounds, other than the piles of trash near the street lights.

Adjust my eyes for night vision, James ordered.

Minor decrease in defensive capability required. Maximum efficiency will be gained through minor adjustments in light collection and minor adjustments in light processing.

Just do it.

James gritted his teeth as burning pain shot through the back of his eyeballs for a second, but when the unpleasant sensation faded, near-daytime light levels had returned.

He'd expected the eerie green of night-vision goggles, but instead, it was as if someone painted glowing paint on all the surfaces. There was something surreal about the whole tableau. For now, it'd work. Even though it'd take some time to fully get used to, he could see everything he needed to in detail.

The trip to the hospital continued, and James arrived at the street right across from the site. Multiple gang tags covered the faded words NORTHWEST PACIFIC HOSPITAL at the entrance to the parking lot.

How many of those bastards have actually kept this as a territory?

James jogged across the street, surveying the area for any sign of his enemy. The sprawling parking lot filled with trash and piles of rock and broken concrete and wood from the hospital gave the alien plenty of places to hide. Aiyn could be anywhere.

I thought this shit wasn't going to be hide and seek?

James let out a low growl, his annoyance building.

Yes, increase power for advanced transformation.

"I'm here," James shouted. "Fucking James Brownstone, Vax Forerunner. The Bogeyman of the Nine Systems Alliance. Come on, Silver Ghost. Come on, Aiyn. I thought you wanted to fucking kill me, and now I have to chase your ass down? Are you too scared to face your monster in the end?"

James ran toward the hospital. Maybe she intended to ambush him inside. Something moved above him, and he skidded to a halt and looked up.

The silver-skinned alien jumped from the fifth floor and hurtled to the ground feet first.

It'd be too much to ask for her to die that way.

Unlikely tactical scenario, Whispy sent.

Yeah, I get that. James chuckled. *I wasn't really asking.*

Aiyn hit the ground in a crouch about ten yards away. She stood, her face as featureless as the police and the other bounty hunters had described.

James threw his arms to the sides. "So here you finally fucking are. All your complicated-ass little schemes. Mercenaries. Nanoform Wendigos. Hiring my fucking girlfriend to get the weapon you were gonna use to kill me." He laughed. "That one's gotta hurt. Spent all that time and money, and she ended up using it to kill that asshole Durand. You might have fancy Nine Systems Alliance nanite shit, but you're not an alien goddess who can predict our every move, are you?"

Kill the enemy, Whispy chanted. *Achieve primary directive.*

Aiyn pointed at him. "I don't know why I feel like telling you, Vax, of all people, but when I was assigned to Earth, I was disappointed."

"Disappointed?"

Maybe this is a good thing. I can get in her head.

Kill the enemy, Whispy complained.

"Yes. The whole point of being a Shepherd is to protect lesser races from dangerous influences or outright invasion." Aiyn lowered her hand. "But Earth and Oriceran... the Alliance knows of no other worlds like them. The magic goes beyond even the rare psionic powers found among some races. Previous Shepherds suspected magic existed on Earth, but they couldn't prove it until the gates opened."

James frowned. "I don't get it. Why does that shit disappoint you?"

"How was I supposed to protect a world with magic? Oricerans and even wizards and witches on this planet can use gates, direct connections in time and space—something we've only seen the Vax do." Aiyn's fingers curled into fists. "But the Vax aren't magic. We know that. We've fought them enough times. Just powerful, and more advanced in a few key areas. I thought I would waste my time on a dangerous planet where if an enemy came, even the Vax, they'd be easily repelled. I thought the Vax adaptation ability would be useless against magic, but when I found out about you, my superiors refused to act; refused to believe the danger. You're a Forerunner who has adapted to magic." She let out an uneven laugh. "How could we stand a chance against something like that? The Alliance has no magical beings."

"Tell me why I should give even the smallest fuck about the Nine Systems Alliance, or that you're not satisfied with your career choice?"

"Of course you wouldn't care, Vax. Your kind has spent a lot of time killing our people and destroying our cities, just like you will eventually. You are a Forerunner. You'll summon more, and they will lay waste to this planet, or Earth and Oriceran will be forced to destroy large chunks of their own planets to defend them. Millions, if not billions, will die."

James slapped a hand on his chest right over his amulet. "I don't give a fuck what the other Vax did. You don't get to come to Earth and fuck with me over shit someone else did. I don't give a fuck who you are or what happened to you. Right now, you're nothing more than a psycho vigilante running around killing people and threatening my friends, so fuck you."

Aiyn stood there in silence for a long moment. "You confound me, Vax, because you shouldn't exist, not as you are. I'll admit certain things about that trouble me, but I've got a solution." She pointed at him again, this time at his chest. "I can see it on you now, you know. The nanites have enhanced my vision. I can see all the energy radiating off the symbiont. Give it up, James Brownstone. That's the only way to prove you're not truly a Vax Forerunner. If you don't, it'll consume your soul and mind eventually anyway. This is your only chance for survival."

"If I didn't have Whispy, I wouldn't have been able to

kick a lot of ass. It's not like your Nine Systems Alliance was there when the Council was fucking people up."

"They don't believe in interference on primitive worlds, even ones as exotic as yours. You can't honestly believe you're that important?"

James shook his head. "Fuck off. Not giving him up. Here's how this shit's gonna go down. You get your own choice. You can go to the little spaceship I'm sure you've gotten hidden in some fucking lake somewhere and fly back to whatever planet you came from, or you can stay and die right here and now."

"Fly back to my planet?" Aiyn stomped forward. "I can't fly back to my planet, *Vax*, because your people overran it. The Vax burned our cities and murdered my people even as they fled in transports. By the time the relief fleet arrived, there was nothing left to do but raze the surface and kill the few remaining Vax." She snickered, but the sound soon grew to a loud laugh. "It doesn't matter. I've already made the sacrifice; merged my body and soul with the nanites. It's enough. All my testing and calibration. All those I've fought have brought me here to face you and destroy you. I will avenge my planet, and save this one from the monster you would become and the other monsters you would summon."

"Might as well get this shit over. I'm not invading Earth, but I'm definitely gonna kill you for everything you've done to me, but especially for Shay, Trey, and Victoria." James' hands clenched, his heart pounding. "You shouldn't have fucked with my woman or my friends."

Yessss, Whispy hissed in his mind. *Sufficient power for advanced transformation.*

The tendrils shot from the amulet and spread over James' chest and arms, forming his metallic silver-green armor. A blade extended from his right arm. Not total coverage, but enough to get the ass-kicking started.

James let out a low growl. "You're gonna die here."

Aiyn charged James. He swung his blade as she closed, but she spun aside, avoiding the blow. She arrived at her target and slammed into him, sending him flying backward.

"I'm going to enjoy taking you down piece by piece, Vax," she shouted.

CHAPTER TWENTY-TWO

James crashed into the wall with a grunt and fell to one knee. The little pain he felt was easy to ignore. Aiyn's revenge was more annoying than threatening so far.

Regeneration levels high. Near maximum adaptation already achieved.

"You have no idea how good that felt, Vax," Aiyn shouted. "I'm beginning to wonder if you're feeling a little doubt in the back of your mind, a little fear that maybe the great Forerunner can't win against a mere Shepherd, even one who's taken such extreme chances. It shouldn't have worked, you know. One hundred thousand to one chance of an integration this successful, but obviously I've been chosen; hand-picked to destroy you. That was why it worked."

James stalked toward her. "Getting a little ahead of yourself, aren't you? Not to mention you're probably going nuts as a side-effect."

Aiyn snapped an arm up. Golden circles appeared

around it, growing brighter over several seconds as the bounty hunter charged her. She released the blast. It exploded against James, sending him spinning through the air, a huge hole in his armor. He landed with a thud in a large pile of fallen concrete and wood.

James' chest throbbed from the crater in it. More tendrils spread out over his body, weaving a new net of armor over his wound. He growled at the pain.

Moderate adaptation achieved, Whispy reported.

"I've spent my entire career studying the Vax," Aiyn explained before firing a few more blasts. The concrete cover saved James from direct hits, nothing more than fragments and dust raining down on him. "I know everything the Alliance has learned about your vicious, evil race."

His pain started to fade and his new layer of armor was completed, even if his wounds weren't fully healed.

James growled and pushed himself up. He shoved a concrete slab out of his way.

Aiyn snorted. "I never thought it'd be easy to kill you, but it's better this way. I'm going to show you something I learned, Vax." She aimed lower. Blue circles around her arm preceded another attack.

The latest energy blast struck his leg and sheared off his armor and the top few layers of tissue. He fell to one knee. Another attack blasted another hole and sent a new spike of pain through him.

James rolled behind the concrete and shook his head to clear some of the pain.

Continuing advanced regeneration, recommend extended advanced mode for improved regeneration.

Even in his pain- and anger-addled mind, he understood the problem. Some people could feed their anger with ease, but he'd become habituated to it, making it more difficult to sustain. Being annoyed wasn't enough for the rage-hungry Whispy Doom.

"My calibration exercises have been pretty useful, don't you think?" Aiyn taunted. "I wasn't sure I could achieve dynamic control, but I'm proving it now, aren't I? Then again, you don't care, do you, Vax? Your kind can portal light-years across the galaxy. That technology is so far ahead of the Alliance, we don't even know how to begin to do it, but what do you do with it? Do you explore new worlds? Do you make new alliances with distant people?" The rocks and concrete fragments crunched under her feet as she stepped forward. "No, you appear out of nowhere to lay waste to planets, which you don't even bother to conquer and make your own. How twisted is that? You kill for the sake of killing. Even a parasite gets something out of their attack."

Even if James hadn't been distracted by anger and growing new armor, skin, and muscles, he wouldn't have bothered with the truth. Did it really matter that the Vax killed because of some sort of pre-emptive defensive religious crusade? It wasn't his fucking problem.

"I'm more convinced than ever that you're some sort of ultimate infiltration unit," Aiyn suggested. "I think the fact that you know you're a Vax but you're convinced you're in control is ridiculous. The Alliance has seen that sort of thing before. Not from the Vax, but if your race is anything, it's adaptable. Maybe you're starting to steal from the races you butcher. Is that it?"

With a new layer of armor established, James rose again and stalked toward Aiyn. She fired another blast, but this time it only singed his armor, even if it enflamed the healing wound underneath.

Heavy adaptation achieved.

The shepherd fired several energy blasts of different colors, each darkening his armor less and inflicting only the barest of stings.

Near maximum adaptation achieved.

"Impressive, Vax," Aiyn hissed. "I see that I didn't spend enough time on calibration after all."

James growled. "Now who's afraid?" He broke into a charge, bringing up his armored fist rather than his blade. She wasn't the only alien there who wanted someone to suffer a little.

Aiyn didn't dodge as James threw his punch. His fist smashed into her head, producing a deep indent and sending her entire body toward a crumbling wall. The shepherd smashed into an exposed internal wall, the rotting wood cracking.

"You're a puppet," she shouted as she hopped to her feet, her head indentation filling in. "Nothing but a body for that thing to control. It's only pretending to let you think."

Kill the enemy, Whispy insisted. *Primary regeneration complete.*

All of his earlier pain had vanished.

"Don't you get it, Vax?" Aiyn continued. "The minute that thing was allowed to attach to you, you ceased to exist." Her arm flowed into a blade. "It'll be fun to dissect your body. Even if I don't live that long, the Alliance can get some use out of it."

James howled in rage and rushed Aiyn again, his blade at the ready this time. He closed the distance and swung, but she parried with her own arm blade and leapt back.

She thrust at him and he slammed his blade on top of hers, knocking it to the ground, where it carved a groove in the dirt- and dust-covered tile floor.

Aiyn retreated, her movements serpentine. "You're even more dangerous than the typical Forerunner. Your minions from Las Vegas can be forgiven, but what of the others like Shay Carson, who know your true nature? You've corrupted them. Made them work against their own planet's interest." She waved her blade. "Have you implanted a symbiont in her, too? Even if you haven't, she seems to know what you are and has chosen herself over her planet. That's even worse than a parasite. I should have killed her when I had the chance, but given what I've seen, she's probably close. I can finish her off soon enough after I'm done with you."

James' already pounding heart kicked into a full gallop, and he bellowed in rage. This bitch came at him and ranted, and then threatened Shay?

Sufficient power for extended advanced transformation.
DO IT!

Armor coated his entire body and sealed his head in a helmet, his field of vision expanding. Claws extended from his hands.

"I will kill you," James roared.

Aiyn scraped her blade against the tile. "That's right, Vax! Show me your true power."

She lunged forward much faster than he'd seen her move before and avoided his swing before jabbing at him several times, but her blade didn't accomplish much. While it didn't bounce off his armor, it also didn't penetrate.

The Shepherd hissed in irritation and somersaulted back several yards on one arm before bringing up both arms and feeding energy into them. James rushed toward her, she had a few seconds to feed her blast.

Her attack struck his armor, exploding and shaking the walls. James stumbled back, only the top layer of armor missing.

Near maximum adaptation achieved, Whispy reported.

"No, no, no," Aiyn shouted. She rushed toward a hole in the wall to the outside.

James hurried after her.

When Aiyn reached the outside, she leapt up a couple of stories and stabbed into the wall with her blade to anchor herself. With a few quick swings and yanks, she ended up on the roof.

Whispy continued his one-track chanting, and his constant waves of joy over his new adaptations fed his host's anger that much more.

James grunted and leapt into the air, his armor helping propel him onto the edge of the roof. He landed with an audible thud, knocking loose several pieces of concrete that tumbled to the ground below.

Aiyn rushed him again, a swirling line of white energy around her blade now. She stabbed at his chest, but the attack bounced off his armor. James replied with a thrust of his own, his blade impaling her.

Disrupt her nanites, he commanded. *Like you did the Wendigo nanoform.*

His opponent thrust at him several more times, but her attacks barely scraped him.

Impossible at this time, Whispy responded. *Nanites stabilized by underlying enemy organic matrix.*

Aiyn yanked herself off James' blade, leaving a huge void where it'd been. The wound started to seal, and she took the opportunity to jump backward off the building, pointing both her arms to feed two different-colored streams of energy into a single blast.

James growled but didn't immediately leap after her.

Her attack discharged and soared toward the roof. It impacted right beneath him, the massive explosion rushing over him and knocking him out of control and into the air. He slammed into the ground seconds later, new holes in his armor and a few wounds underneath.

Regeneration in progress.

James ignored his damage and wounds and raised his own arm, ready to demonstrate his own energy cannon. Aiyn's head twitched several times, and she fell to her knees just past another hole leading inside the hospital.

I fucking win.

The amulet chanting for death in his head, James took a slow, deliberate step toward the downed alien, growling the entire way. He was going to slice her into so many pieces she'd never regenerate. It'd be more satisfying that way.

No one fucking threatens Shay.

CHAPTER TWENTY-THREE

When James closed half the distance, Aiyn abruptly jumped up and shook her head. "I should have known from the beginning it wouldn't be enough. I've got nothing left to lose. I might as well go all-out."

James stepped forward. "Die already."

"I'm surprised by how much of yourself you can maintain even now, Vax, especially considering how much trouble I've had keeping myself together."

Ripples appeared all over Aiyn's silver body and joined together. A bright white sheen surrounded her.

James growled and raised his blade. She'd gotten in a few good hits at the beginning, but now he had the upper hand. Her tricks wouldn't save her.

Aiyn zoomed forward, her movement a blur. She slammed into James before he even registered what was going on and sent him crashing through two walls. A concrete support pillar stopped his flight, but he bounced off and hit the ground.

James stood just in time to be on the receiving end of a powerful jump-kick that knocked him off his feet again. This time he smashed through the concrete support pillar like it was a few inches of wood. Part of the floor above collapsed, burying him in a pile of concrete and wood.

After a few quick thrusts and pushes, James crawled out of the pile, his armor pitted in several places but his wounds only stinging despite the high level of force involved. If he'd been in advanced mode, maybe the attack would have been more effective, but each failed penetration gave him more time to regenerate underneath.

Aiyn's head and limbs twitched. More ripples appeared, and her light intensified.

"I-I-I'm going to kill you, V-Vax," she stuttered.

Aiyn charged James again, her speed nearly impossible to track. She threw a powerful uppercut that connected with his helmet and launched him toward the ceiling.

Her follow-up was a two-handed overhead slam while he was still in the air that sent him crashing into the ground so hard, he cracked the tile and ended up embedded several inches, mild pain radiating through his body.

Minor damage, Whispy reported.

The shepherd leapt on top of him, formed her other arm into a blade, and started stabbing with wild abandon. Each blow flaked off some armor and stung, but after a few attacks, additional small tendrils spread to repair the armor. James' enemy simply couldn't hurt him fast enough and deep enough to beat his current passive healing.

Some of Whispy's joy dimmed.

Near maximum adaptation achieved. Utility of current enemy limited. Kill enemy.

James swung his arm and knocked Aiyn off with a blow that sent her flailing backward. She hit the ground and hopped up into a crouch, swaying unsteadily, body rippling and still bathed in light.

"You can't win," Aiyn yelled. "I won't let you win. I've been chosen. Something like *you* can't win. You don't have the creativity to win. You're just a meat puppet for a fake parasitic brain."

He didn't respond. Her words barely registered, drowned out by his residual burning anger and the drumbeat of death demands from the symbiont. At least this time, they were in complete agreement about the best course of action.

Aiyn had the advantage of speed for the moment, and if a blade wouldn't work, it was time for something harder to dodge.

James lifted his arms and extended a second blade on his other arm. He fed energy into both. Green sparks rushed over his blades, building in frequency and intensity.

"Oh, that was a mistake, Vax." Aiyn's blades reverted to normal arms. A veritable rainbow of colored circles pulsed over them as she funneled energy into her own blast. "I don't have to live. I only have to make sure that you die."

An audible crackle filled the air as his energy built, some of his sparks blowing chunks off the walls. He couldn't even make his enemy out behind the bright ball of energy in front of her.

The seconds ticked by, and he kept feeding more and more energy into the attack.

The shepherd fired first, but James released his twin beams an instant later.

Aiyn's attack exploded around him, producing a huge, billowing cloud of debris. He careened through the air, dizzy, some layers of his armor burned or scored off, but almost no holes or wounds.

James lost track of time until he crashed into the hard ground, wood, concrete, and dust raining down around him. His time in the air felt like minutes, even though his addled mind understood it to be mere seconds.

Near maximum adaptation achieved from cross-sampling synergy, Whispy reported. *Minimal damage. Regeneration in progress.*

His health was irrelevant. The concern was the enemy. She needed to die.

James stood and stalked through the cloud of dust choking the area in search of his silver-skinned prey. He spun toward a nearby humanoid form, only to realize it was a chance configuration of dust and not Aiyn.

Ten seconds of searching passed before he spotted her lying immobile on the ground, a huge hole in her chest. A few more inches on either side and he would have split her body in two.

Even though Aiyn didn't appear to be breathing, that didn't quell his bloodlust. With her modifications, it was unclear that she needed to breathe. Total annihilation would be necessary to ensure her death and end her harassment once and for all.

James lifted his foot, ready to advance, but stopped when he spotted something else.

Aiyn's face was no longer featureless. The top layer of

silver was gone, replaced by smooth blue skin and yellow eyes. She coughed several times, viscous gray fluid coming out instead of blood.

His only response was a long, low, angry growl. The insane zealot had been after him for so long. Now he only needed to finish her off.

Aiyn managed to lift her head. "I'm dead anyway, even if the nanites can stitch me back together. It doesn't matter, but do you think you've won, Vax?" She chuckled, her eyes half-closed. "I've tried to prevent collateral damage and honor the Shepherd oaths, but you've left me no choice. It's lucky you picked a neighborhood filled with parasites. Some losses are inevitable in war, I suppose." The nimbus around her grew even more blinding.

Her threat against the innocent people around the hospital barely registered in his angry clouded mind. Shay and his friends—that was all he cared about. That was why Aiyn needed to die.

Kill the enemy, he thought in almost perfect unison with Whispy Doom.

James lifted his arms again, this time forcing his thoughts toward something other than beams. The now-familiar bright green sparks appeared on his arms, but instead of concentrating them there, he fed the energy between his arms as Aiyn had done. A tiny green dot soon grew into a small orb of energy, then to something nearly the size of his chest.

It was time to take Whispy's advice and kill the enemy by getting rid of every last piece of her body. Complete and total destruction.

Don't ever even think about fucking with my woman.

With a roar, James released his attack. The massive green energy ball crashed into the downed Aiyn. A massive shockwave knocked him back and blew out the surrounding walls and support pillars.

The wooden walls became burning particles in the heated wind, but the concrete pillar cracked, with many small pieces shooting from it as if some giant had walked up and struck it with a massive hammer.

Maximum adaptation to own attack, Whispy reported.

When the dust cleared, James crawled back to his feet with a grunt. He marched forward as he sought any sign of his enemy, but there was only a blackened crater where her body once lay.

Need to be sure.

James stared at the crater, growling, almost expecting Aiyn to regenerate and pop back in to taunt him, but there was nothing. He stood there for a good minute, waiting, his anger drifting away and his heart slowing.

No body or stray silver specks remained, only a burnt crater, smoke, and dust.

It was over. He'd achieved his goal: total obliteration of the enemy.

The amulet's whispers quieted, replaced by satisfaction slowly suffusing through his mind and the rest of his body as the tension drifted out of his muscles.

James' claws and blades retracted and the tendrils of armor retreated as well, which left him a shirtless man in ripped pants. Now that the battle was over there was residual pain, but not much. Most of his earlier deep wounds had already healed.

"Total fucking victory, huh?" James muttered to himself.

If he'd met the shepherd before achieving advanced mode, would he have had a chance to convince her to leave him alone? Given everything she'd done, he doubted that.

It didn't matter if it was street thugs in LA or interplanetary assassins, the rule remained the same: don't fuck with him if you wanted to live. At least there weren't hundreds of Nine Systems Alliance people waiting to come after him, based on what Aiyn had told him.

James surveyed the area. The building hadn't been destroyed, but half of it was a smoldering pile of debris.

At least I managed to only destroy half a building, Shay, he thought.

Recommend quiescence for continued cellular regeneration, Whispy reported. *Maximum efficiency in current form has nearly been reached. Additional adaptation remains possible, but recommend genetic and cellular modifications for future Forerunner transformation achievement. Possible interface capability issues may arise due to local lifeform genetic code interference.*

James let out a dark chuckle. Whispy had made him more human all those years ago, and now he was bitching about him being too human. He was more interested in something pragmatic.

Will Forerunner mode make me stronger? Tougher?

Yes. Forerunner transformation required for primary directive.

Which is?

James had asked many times before, only to be blown off by the stubborn necklace, but if it were ready to take him to his final transformation, it wouldn't have much choice but to tell him what it wanted.

Primary directive...error, Whispy admitted. *Conflicting primary directives. Non-resolvable.*

List them, James demanded.

Primary directive: Achieve full local tactical domination appropriate for symbiont matrix sharing with Vax Vanguard and initiate tracking pulse to summon Vanguard to target planet for cleansing.

Primary directive: Destroy all Vax symbionts.

James let out a loud laugh. "You did it, Mom and Dad. You hacked the symbiont. He hates himself so much he didn't even want to think about what you told him to do, and he's been erroring out and letting me stay in control ever since. I don't even know if he could take control even if he wanted to."

Does Forerunner mode require tracking pulse to be sent? James sent.

No. Pulse requires full tactical control by enhancement symbiont.

James smirked. *But even if you can do that, you can't have control because I won't hand over the keys.*

Link error acknowledged.

We're never going to call them, James sent. *We'll never achieve that primary directive, but here's a truth for you, Whispy. We're never going to achieve the other primary directive either. You and me, we're going to stay together, because someday one of those Nine Systems Alliance bastards might come back, or even one of these Vanguards, and we're going to turn into a Forerunner and destroy them. We're going to reduce them to nothing, just like we did with the shepherd. Do I make myself fucking clear?*

Whispy beamed back excitement at the possibility. Apparently, in the end, he didn't care as long as he got to help the bounty hunter kick ass. James didn't mind. That he could work with.

Go ahead and make the modifications, but maintain my humanity, James sent.

That will extend time required for modifications and lower efficiency.

James snorted. *I'm not Aiyn. I'm not giving up everything. You made me mostly human when I was a kid, and I'm staying that way. Do what I say.*

Entering quiescence and initiating long-term cellular and genetic modification, the amulet replied.

James didn't feel any pain. Every other Whispy modification had hurt. Maybe he was still keeping his humanity after all, or maybe the amulet would spend months doing the modifications. At that moment, James didn't really give a shit.

He brushed some of the dust and grime off his exposed torso before heading toward the edge of the property, unsure if there was still interference.

"Heather, can you hear me?"

No response.

James reached up and patted his ear. No earpiece left. Not surprising, considering all the damage and transformation.

Aiyn had been defeated. Not just defeated, completely obliterated. The future was wide open for James, but there was at least one outstanding problem he needed to handle that shouldn't require him to blow up anything.

"Damn it. Maybe it would have been fucking epic to propose before the battle after all." James' stomach rumbled. "Shit. We'll grab some In-N-Out tonight and go to Jessie Rae's tomorrow morning. I can figure something out after that."

CHAPTER TWENTY-FOUR

James finished his shower. He turned off the water and stepped out into the steam-filled bathroom, feeling refreshed now that he'd gotten the grime and dust off him. Having a hospital collapse on a man was a good way to dirty him up, let alone getting knocked through walls.

She did all that, and in the end, it wasn't worth shit. Don't know if that means her plan was weak, or I've just gotten that strong.

James toweled off. He'd brought his change of clothes with him into the bathroom with the knowledge that if he walked into the bedroom without his clothes, Shay might jump him, especially after the night they'd had. As fun as the idea was, if they started something while they were still in Los Angeles, they would never make it to Las Vegas.

Spontaneity had been stuck in his head since their drive back from the hospital. All the relationship podcasts mentioned how important it was, but then they talked about proposals as something that should be planned in most cases. It confused him, and the whole subject was confusing enough already.

Anna's advice argued the opposite, and something about it felt right at gut level. Maybe it was because she was hundreds of years old and not human, or because he'd actually talked to her face-to-face, he trusted her opinion.

Even though he wasn't sure any particular opportunity would arise in Las Vegas for a solid fucking epic proposal, spending a couple of days there on a whim in a place that catered to people's spontaneous whims sounded like a better idea for stumbling into proposal possibilities that might be epic than sitting around in Los Angeles watching the same shows and going to the same restaurants.

It wasn't that LA didn't have plenty of venues, but it had just been too much a part of his KISS routine for his entire life. Everything about LA felt comfortable and safe to him, as opposed to Vegas. He'd been there many times, but the truth was, the city still held many surprises for him.

With a quick shimmy, James donned his boxers and then his pants. He grabbed a t-shirt next. They weren't going to Vegas to kick ass, so he could be casual and not worry about a heavy tactical outfit.

I swear that if some fucking genetically-engineered magic monster pops up, I'll beat it down the first fucking day and we'll continue on our mini-vacation.

After James put on his clothes, he stepped out of the bathroom. The steam billowed out into the cooler bedroom where Shay sat cross-legged on the bed.

She cradled James' phone between her shoulder and neck as she held up her own phone and typed in a message. "Yeah, yeah. Thanks, Mack. After everything that happened, I think just letting him relax for a couple of days might be helpful, but I'll make sure he gets you all the information you need before the end of the week, and I'll let him know. Talk to you later. Again, thanks for all your help." She set her phone down and held James' phone out to him.

James frowned. "Why didn't you tell me Mack was calling?"

"Because I thought you could use an hour where you didn't have to worry about Aiyn Noraz Hal and her bullshit. That bitch rode you for months, and you shouldn't have to immediately care about her, considering all that shit you just went through."

James narrowed his eyes. "Is she back? Did she regenerate after all?"

Shay shook her head. "Nah, that was just Mack getting basic information about what went down. Your terse text to them wasn't very descriptive."

"I was in a hurry."

"Don't I know it! He also said that because you blew her up completely, there might be some difficulty getting the bounty processed, but he's pushing for it based on your record with the department and city. I doubt the LAPD and the City and County of Los Angeles want to stiff James Brownstone, especially when the LAPD was the one begging you to go after the Silver Ghost in the first place."

"I don't care that much about the money, but I'm glad to hear it." James looked down at his phone. "Let's go to Vegas."

Shay's brows lifted. "Vegas? In the middle of the night? Why?"

"Because tomorrow I want to get some Jessie Rae's." James shrugged. "I earned that shit, and I want to eat as soon as I can."

"Jessie Rae's won't be open by the time we get there, though," Shay replied warily. "You know that, right?"

"Then we'll stay overnight. If there's no room in the loft, we can get a hotel. If we're already in Vegas, I won't have to drive there tomorrow. I don't want to think about bounties or alien shit. I just want to relax with you and eat some barbeque."

A faint smirk appeared on her face. "A hotel in Vegas, huh?"

Why does she look like that? Am I missing something?

"Yeah, not like they're hard to find," James replied. "If the LAPD needs shit from me about Aiyn over the next few days, they can just call me." He frowned. "You didn't tell them the truth, did you? That'll just complicate everything, and then it won't be over for a while."

Shay typed another message into her phone. "Nope. As far as they're concerned, the Silver Ghost was just some strange vigilante whose identity may never be known. I think the big fucking crater you left was enough closure for them. Let's be honest—they were pissed because cops got hurt and they thought there was going to be a gang war. You solved both their problems."

"You think they'll find anything? Like a nanite or some weird radiation or shit?"

Shay considered that for a few seconds and shrugged. "I'm sure they'll have forensics, conventional and magical, sweep the area, but it's not your problem even if they do find nanites or something, now is it? You didn't say one thing about who and what the Ghost was, you just went after her at their request."

"You don't think it'll cause problems with the government?"

"Maybe, but it'll be more of a problem for the LAPD than you. That's one of the things I'm having Peyton watch, and that's what I've been writing him about for the last few minutes." Shay set her phone down. "He noticed unusual military activity that apparently started in the last few days. It might be a coincidence, but I don't know. Given that we know the government is involved in this alien shit, I don't want to ignore it totally, but I figure it's not something we'll have to worry about in the next couple of days if you want to spend time in Vegas."

"Was this military shit in LA?" James replied. "Maybe they were planning to go after the Silver Ghost themselves."

"No, that's just it. The activity was all over the United States; unusually high deployment considering we don't have any major wars going on. Peyton's in some DOD systems, but he's scaled back because we don't want to bring the entire government down on us. Officially, the Pentagon's claiming they're doing some sort of country-wide readiness exercise, but there's a lot of fancy and expensive equipment being moved around, and it's not a previously scheduled exercise. There's also some hint of PDA involvement, but it's dangerous to poke around in their systems because Peyton doesn't have a good way to counter magical hacking." Shay snickered. "Yeah, speaking of that, it's probably going to get annoying in the future.

Eventually, both of us are going to need magical types to help Peyton and Heather."

James sat on the edge of the bed. "I'll worry about that shit when the time comes. For now, though, it doesn't sound like this military thing has anything to do with me, or they wouldn't have activated people all over the country for it. They would have just done shit like Aiyn, either near Los Angeles or Las Vegas, so they could get at me if necessary."

"That's what I've been thinking, but it's hard to be too paranoid when we've just gotten done taking down an alien who pretended to be a billionaire for years and did everything from sending a fake Wendigo after you to hiring me and one of my archnemeses at the same time on a tomb-raiding job."

James grinned as he pulled a pair of socks out of his drawer. "You see? That was her problem. All that complicated shit kept blowing up in her face. Going to someone and just beating them down—not a lot of moving parts in that plan to fail."

"Oh, don't get too full of yourself, Captain KISS," Shay replied. "Your latest takedown required two hackers running around planting false messages on the internet to lure an alien to a particular abandoned hospital at a specific time. This wasn't exactly you having Tyler call someone and getting them to agree to a pay-per-view."

"Whatever. The principle's the same." James grunted.

Shay's expression softened. "And what do you plan to do if the military comes after you? Could you really fire on them?"

"We don't know they're coming at me."

"But what would you do?"

James frowned. "Get away, I guess. If they didn't kill me, that would give me a chance to find someone to help me. Let's just hope it doesn't come to that." He grimaced. "Shit, better set out extra food and water for Thomas before we go. I was worried about him and the doggie door, but he's fitting okay even with the extra weight."

"If you're worried, you could always have Mack watch him. I mean, your dog isn't exactly a handful. He spends most of his time just sitting by chairs and relaxing."

James shook his head. "I figure we'll be in Vegas a day or two max. Just a quick trip. Don't want to inconvenience Mack, and it's good for Thomas to remember that I have to leave every now and again."

"Vegas it is." Shay stared at James for a moment as if carefully examining his face and trying to memorize it. "Okay, then." She hopped off the bed. "I'll throw some shit in a bag." She headed toward the closet. "Quickie wedding chapels aren't fucking epic," she murmured a little too loudly for it to not be on purpose.

James blinked.

Don't know if she'll be pissed that we're not doing that shit.

CHAPTER TWENTY-FIVE

Shay let out a long yawn as they headed up I-15 North, their headlights cutting through the thick darkness. As tired as she might be, the one advantage of driving in the middle of the night was that there weren't a lot of cars on the road. She didn't remember seeing one in the last hour, but most people weren't crazy enough to go on late-night runs to Vegas so they could have their preferred barbeque the next day.

He did earn it. Too bad he couldn't have picked a local place for his reward. How the hell does traveling to another city fit into the Brownstone KISS philosophy?

Shay smirked and glanced his way. Apparently, the only things allowed to be complicated in James' life were his woman and his barbeque.

I'm glad I don't have to make him choose between me and the barbeque. He might choose the barbeque!

James hadn't said much in the last hour, staying in what Shay hoped was thoughtful silence about a pending proposal. She'd tried not to harass him about it, but her patience was running thin. A long engagement was one thing, but she already knew he wanted to marry her, so the clock was ticking in her mind.

Then again, how much could a woman complain when she was the one who had set up the difficulty to begin with?

Would it really be so bad if he just got it over with? It's not like I've ever been the type of woman who wanted a big, impressive wedding with the fancy dress and all that shit, so it's not like I need a proposal like that. What was I thinking when I said that to him?

Maybe it was a mistake to give him that speech about his proposal needing to be fucking epic. It's pretty fucking epic for James Brownstone to want to take that step at all. Or I could propose to him? Fuck, I don't know.

James is right. Love is hard.

Shay sneaked a glance at him. He wasn't smiling or frowning. Instead, he kept his attention on the road, his brow furrowed as if he was deep in thought.

Maybe this shit has nothing to do with me at all. Even if that Aiyn bitch had it coming and was going psycho anyway, he might still have let her get in his head, or he's worried about that Vanguard crap. I need to make sure he doesn't need to worry about it and let him know I'll always have his back no matter what.

Shay licked her lips. "Hey, we should talk."

James nodded. "You're right. I do want to make sure you understood that I want to eat at least two meals at Jessie Rae's tomorrow. Maybe three, depending on how hungry I am, and I've noticed I'm always really hungry after I've gone through a lot of regeneration. The fight the other day involved a lot of it. Aiyn got in some good hits, I'll give her that."

"You want to eat a lot of barbeque? Is that seriously what you've been thinking about for the last hour?"

James nodded. "Thinking about all the different kinds I want to have. I want to go all-out. Really go to town."

"Fine." Shay chuckled. "That's fine, James. You earned it. I don't hate barbeque, you know. I just want to mix things up a little more than you do. As much as I love pizza, I couldn't eat it as often as you eat barbeque, but that's not what I wanted to talk about."

"Sure, okay. What did you want to talk about? Alison's summer plans?"

"Not yet. It's about you. You never told me if you're okay." Shay gave him a warm smile. "I know you're the baddest Vax in the whole damned town and all that, but I still wanted to make sure. You know you can always talk to me."

James grunted. "I'm fine. Like I said, she got some good hits in, but I can't find any cuts or anything. Whispy's doing his thing, but he also didn't try and stop me when I pulled him off. I didn't need a healing potion either. I will say all this improved regeneration's gonna save me money. Shit piles up, you know. I won't always be in extended or extended advanced, but it's still gonna help."

"I'm... Okay, that's good. I mean, it's good that you've regenerated and aren't seriously hurt." Shay gave him an exasperated sigh. "But that's not the shit I was talking about. I meant your feelings. Your mind, and all that. I just wanted to make sure you weren't sliding into a Brownstone brood."

The confused expression James gave her almost made her laugh in his face, but she called on her self-control to stop herself. That would only complicate things. The last thing she needed to do was make James question being honest about his feelings.

"My feelings?" James rumbled. "I feel good. I fucking got that bitch off our backs, and I'm going to Jessie Rae's with you. What's to feel bad about? I'm sure Mack will work out that bounty shit, so I'm not worried about any of..." His hands tightened around the wheel. "Son of a bitch!"

"James? What's going on?"

"I might just be seeing things, but after today, I damned well want to be sure." His gaze cut between the side and rearview mirrors. "Look behind us and tell me what you see. If it's nothing, then we'll continue to have a good night. If not, time for some more ass-kicking."

Shay's stomach tightened, and she turned her head.

The highway lacked lights, but the truck's taillights were on, keeping the area behind them from being totally dark—and that was where the problem lay. Complete blackness would have been more comforting, in a way.

The slight illumination of the taillights highlighted the bare shadow of a large form floating about twenty feet off the ground. Some of the light bent in wrong ways, outlining something much larger than the truck and roughly triangular. If she hadn't been looking for it explicitly, she might not have noticed.

"I see it," Shay breathed. "Damn it. Come on, already."

"Exactly." James pulled off the highway and slammed on the brakes. The strange optical phenomenon disappeared, but the entire truck rattled and shook as if a huge train was passing right over them.

Shay checked her gun in her holster and sighed. "Sometimes it's just luck, you know? But if it's Aiyn again, she has to be weaker than the last time. Much weaker."

"I don't think it's her. Call it my gut instinct." James reached into his shirt and yanked off the spacer behind his amulet. He grimaced as the bonding took place. "Fuck luck, and fuck whatever's after us. I wanted some time off with you, and I wanted my fucking barbeque."

They both stepped out of the truck. Nothing but scrubland and shrubs around them that they could see, but the plants fluttered at the touch of a hot wind seemingly coming from above with no obvious source.

What the fuck is that?

James and Shay craned their necks upwards. Again, the stray light reaching above them from the truck highlighted a huge spectral form in the darkness.

The form shimmered for a few seconds and a thin silver triangular aircraft revealed itself, utterly silent despite the obvious blue-white gases coming out of the bottom.

What was with the rumble earlier? Were they fucking with us on purpose?

Shay's stomach tightened as she stared up at the bottom of the ship. She pointed at some familiar symbols on the bottom. "They aren't exactly the same as the thing on your amulet, but they are very damned similar, plus similar to some other alien symbols I've found in my research."

"What are you saying? It's the Vax? If it's them, I'm gonna fucking beat their asses all the way to the center of the Earth."

Shay shrugged. "Your guess is as good as mine."

"No, it's not them." James snorted. "Thanks to Aiyn, I know it's not them."

"Huh? What do you mean? How do you know?"

James pointed above. "She ranted about it. The Vax use some sort of portals, it sounded like, rather than ships. Technological portals rather than magic. Sounded like the Alliance didn't really understand them."

"Huh. I was kind of wondering why similar symbols popped up in different contexts. Maybe it's more like a common alphabet or something? That would explain a lot." Shay smiled for a few seconds before wincing.

I'm getting lost in cool archaeology and linguistics when there's most likely an alien ship right above us, and I doubt they're tourists looking for the nearest barbeque joint.

James laughed. "No. I know exactly who these assholes are. Don't bother pulling a gun. Bet you your phone has no signal all of a sudden. I should have expected this shit."

"Yeah, once I realized there was a ship above us, I kind of got that a handgun wouldn't be helpful." Shay pulled out her phone to check.

No signal. Even if this part of the highway wasn't great for reception, she tended to at least get some bars.

Shay groaned. "They've got us locked down. Fuck."

"No, fuck them." James slapped his chest. "Fuck you, Nine Systems Alliance. You want to kill me, then go ahead and do it, because all I want to do is go get some fucking barbeque with my girlfriend because your psycho shepherd was about to nuke half of Los Angeles because she was pissed about something I didn't even do to her. Oh, and that's after she murdered a bunch of people and fucked up my friends and the cops after some weird nanite bonding shit. Is this what you do?" He shook his fist. "You're so damned worried about protecting Earth from alien invasions. How the fuck was what went down not an alien invasion? So, you hear that? My Vax Forerunner ass just stopped an alien invasion by the Nine Systems alliance. So either fucking kill me or get the hell out of our way so I can get to Vegas, get some sleep, and get some damned barbeque after having fun with Shay."

Glad to see he's got solid priorities.

"Okay... That's not the way I would have handled this, but I doubt they can hear you up the—" The triangular craft began to descend. "Or maybe they can."

James and Shay exchanged looks, and he shrugged.

Shay laughed. "I can't believe this shit is happening. You're either the unluckiest bastard on the planet or the luckiest."

Despite the fact they might be about to face multiple Aiyns, Shay found herself more fascinated than afraid. After months of worrying about the elusive alien huntress and finally finding relief after her defeat, she just couldn't bring herself to worry at that moment. Also, James' arrogant defiance was inspiring in its own way.

Nothing was more Brownstone than him yelling at an alien ship about his right to eat barbeque and have sex with his girlfriend.

The ship landed to the side of the road, and the engines cut out. They scorched the ground.

"It's a close encounter now," Shay muttered. "Assholes should watch it so they don't start a fire."

James stomped toward the ship, and Shay fell in behind him, still more curious than worried.

White light bathed the body of the ship, illuminating the entire area. The ship wasn't huge, close to the size of an average Learjet. There were no obvious weapons, but Shay couldn't even begin to figure out what she might be looking for, given some of the technology and abilities displayed by Aiyn.

As the Silver Ghost, she could fire energy blasts from her arms. The ship might have all sorts of hidden projectors or gun ports or an expanding energy field that blasted from the body.

The side of the ship slid open, and a metal ramp extended quickly from the nearly open doorway to the ground with a quiet whir.

James stopped about five yards away and crossed his arms over his chest, scowling at the opening in the ship.

I'm honestly not sure if he's more pissed about us potentially being attacked or his barbeque run getting fucked up.

A single blue-skinned yellow-eyed humanoid male emerged from the ship clad in a loose blue-white uniform, a wide belt with several pouches hanging around his waist.

Shay narrowed her eyes at an obvious sidearm in a holster, and some worry crept in.

Well, maybe it's not a sidearm. Maybe it's his space stapler, and he's a space accountant who just wants to talk to us about term life insurance.

The alien held up his hands in an obvious gesture of de-escalation. He cleared his throat. "You are James Brownstone and Shay Carson?"

His accent was odd, but that wasn't surprising, given

the situation. Shay was just happy he had the technology or the ability to speak a language she could understand. For all she knew, Aiyn spent fifty years studying Earth languages before arriving.

James frowned. "Yeah, I'm James Brownstone. You're the same species as, let's see, Sentry 7921, Shepherd 2nd Class Aiyn Noraz Hal. If you're here to try to arrest me or whatever, fuck off. I stand by everything I said and did. She was the one fucking with me, and plenty of humans too."

The alien stared at James, a puzzled expression on his face. At least that was how Shay interpreted it, but she couldn't be certain if he was close enough to human in psychology that his facial expressions implied the same mental states.

"And you killed her," the alien man stated. There was no accusation in the flat tone.

"I defended myself after months of her hounding the people I care about and me." James dropped his arms and fisted his hands. "If you want to get in line for a beat down, go ahead. I'm damned pissed now, and I could use the exercise."

Shay watched in silence, awed by James' continued defiance, given the situation. If the alien had any sort of weapons on his ship, they might not be able to counter them. Even a good old Earth fighter plane could destroy the truck with ease from miles away with a missile.

"Aiyn..." the alien began. "There are problems with things that have occurred. Some of this was our fault. We underestimated how certain things would progress, given the information we had available."

James didn't say anything, but he did unclench his hands.

The alien gestured to James. "Our policy of minimal interference except in defense against other advanced species has become...strained because of the complicated nature of Earth and Oriceran. Obviously, Aiyn has said and done a lot to further complicate this particular situation. We were worried she might try something abrupt since she recently cut off contact with us, and audits of certain datastreams indicated she was doing things she shouldn't. We came as soon as possible, but..."

"But what?" Shay asked.

"James Brownstone, you are a Vax Forerunner, are you not?"

James shrugged. "Among other things. It's kinda down on the list after bounty hunter and barbeque enthusiast."

"Prince of Pec-town," Shay added.

James gave her an odd look, and she smirked back. Something about the situation was too strange to not have a little fun. If she was about to be killed by some alien, she at least wanted to have a fun time with her man for the last few minutes.

This alien seems more confused than we are.

The alien looked at James and Shay. His expression suggested he didn't understand a single thing either of them had just said. "You're an anomaly, Mr. Brownstone. You shouldn't exist, and that makes it hard to decide how to proceed."

James ripped open his shirt to reveal the bonded amulet. The alien stepped back, his gaze locked on his chest.

"It doesn't control me," James explained. "I control it. I don't feel like I should have to give you my life story, but my parents died making sure I didn't have to become a Vax Forerunner and join in their wars. I grew up on Earth, and consider it my home. I use my abilities to take down bounties and other assholes who come after my friends and me. If your shepherd had left me alone, she'd still be alive and running her charity, but she couldn't stop herself."

"We tracked her energy signature and observed the last portion of your fight." The alien continued to stare at James' chest, tension lining his blue face. "We understand that our shepherd had become unstable even before her illegal and dangerous nanobonding procedure, but you still have to understand this from our perspective. You are an incredibly dangerous being, both individually and as a potential summoner of your species."

"Meaning what?"

The alien's gaze flicked to the ship. "The fact that you're a bonded Vax with free will is interesting, but I'm not certain the Alliance can allow you to stay on this planet—not to mention the potential value that could come from studying you."

James shook his head. "I'm not leaving Earth."

"To be clear, I'm trying to be polite, but I'm also not suggesting you have much choice in the matter."

Shay stepped in front of James and glared at the alien. "I don't care if you're the Emperor of the Nine Systems or whatever. You're not coming to our planet and our country and kidnapping one of our people. Fuck off."

"But he's *not* one of your people. He's a Vax." The alien blinked, the light reflecting from his yellow eyes. "He's as inhuman as a gnome or a Kilomea. Even more so, really, because at least those species have some connection to your world's history and people."

James' mouth twisted into a hungry grin and his hands twitched. "What are you going to do? Aiyn did all that, as you called it, 'illegal nanobonding shit,' and she still didn't win. I've already adapted to all sorts of attacks from your technology. You wouldn't stand a chance against me if I got serious."

The alien shook his head. "I doubt you could survive an anti-matter torpedo at point-blank range, Mr. Brown-stone, and there aren't any other humans around for a long distance to be at risk."

Fuck. This is going south in a big way. We need to do something.

Shay swallowed, wondering if there were any more aliens on the ship. Without the nanite procedure, she doubted the alien could last more than a few seconds against her and James, but if he had backup, that'd just bring on an attack, and they'd still end up dust in a crater just like Aiyn.

An odd hum filled the air, and they all turned toward the source. A small dot appeared and expanded into a portal. Then another appeared, and another.

What now?

The alien spun to each portal as it opened, confusion on his face.

James looked more annoyed than confused. "I can't wait until this fucking night is over."

Twelve portals appeared. A moment later a US Army soldier in an exoskeleton and AR goggles holding a railgun emerged from the first. Others poured out of the rest of the portals with different weapons—railguns, rifles, and rocket launchers.

Two portals joined to form a larger portal, and a few seconds later a tank rolled out.

A roar sounded overhead as something screamed by; fighter planes from the sound of them.

"What the ever-loving fuck is going on?" James yelled.

Shay took in all the new arrivals, not sure if having the military here was a good thing or bad thing.

The alien stood rigidly and locked his attention on James.

Worried he's going to go all Forerunner on your ass? You should be.

The military deployment took under a minute, by the end, sixty heavily-armed men surrounded James, Shay, and the alien, supplemented by four tanks and an unknown number of planes flying nearby. A small group of wizards and witches emerged from the portal, their wands pointed at the alien.

The portals closed one by one, with a final one lingering. A suited and familiar old man stepped out: Senator Johnston. He walked toward James.

"I'm glad this showdown happened in the United States," the senator offered with a quick glance at the alien. "Things could have gotten dicey otherwise, son. I'm just going to get this out of the way. We've been spying on you magically for the last few hours. Be pissed all you want, but in this case, I think it helps us both."

James looked down at his exposed bonded amulet. So much for his big secret from the government.

The senator looked at James and the alien. "So, James, now I understand a little more about you, though to be honest, we'd already pretty much figured out you weren't from around here after the Council incident." He turned toward the alien. "And Miss Carson's right. Mr. Brownstone, regardless of what planet he was born on, is legally a United States citizen. I don't know how you run things in your—what was it called?—Nine Systems Alliance, but in America, we don't take kindly to foreigners kidnapping our citizens. It makes us rather angry, in fact."

The alien looked the senator up and down. "Who are you? Are you authorized to speak for the government of the United States?"

"I'm Senator Angus Johnston, and I'm currently authorized to speak on behalf of the United States, yes, and the North Atlantic Treaty Organization, so keep in mind that what you do in the next few minutes may result in war with a lot of very well-armed nations." He clucked his tongue. "I know what you're thinking, 'Oh, well, these primitive apes can't do much to us.' Keep in mind, my alien friend, that we've got nukes and we've got magic. I think that'll be enough to at least cause you a little pain. And if push comes to shove, we've got treaties with the Oricerans for strategic-level magic. We get our hands on a little sample, we can probably come knocking on your door."

"You misunderstand." The alien's face twitched. "The Nine Systems Alliance is protecting Earth. Yes, there was an issue with a rogue operative, but it's been…handled."

The senator chuckled and nodded. "Yeah, the Silver Ghost was an alien. Interesting how that worked out."

James grunted. "She had it in for me for a while; for months. The Silver Ghost shit was just the latest version."

"I see." The senator smiled at the alien. "From what I've seen, my alien friend, that problem was handled because of James Brownstone, not because of you, so why should I trust anything you say?"

The alien narrowed his eyes. "No matter how much you think you can trust him, he's a Vax Forerunner. His people are conquerors."

The senator laughed. "Welcome to Earth. Everyone's descended from someone who conquered someone. Now, of course, James will have to share a few details with the US government for his safety, but that doesn't change the fact that we're not going to let you take him off this planet. Quite frankly, my alien friend, after this incident, if your government doesn't establish some sort of formal, even if secret, diplomatic ties with the major countries on Earth, we'd consider that...troublesome and potentially a hostile act."

The roar of another jet passing overhead filled the night. Some of the soldiers had their weapons trained on the alien, others on the ship. All four tanks pointed their main cannons at the ship.

Shay continued watching in silence, utterly surprised by the events unfolding in front of her.

The alien looked around and frowned. "James Brownstone might be the doom of your world. You don't understand how dangerous he is."

Senator Johnston shook his head. "No, it's the exact opposite. I understand *precisely* how dangerous he is. He might be an alien sonofabitch from an entire race of sonsofbitches, but he's our sonofabitch, you understand? So I think you should get back in your little ship, fly up, and contact whoever gives you orders and explain that James Brownstone will not be joining you for a tour."

"You're all fools." The alien pivoted on his heel and headed toward his ship.

"Wait," James called.

What the hell is he doing? He better not have let that bastard convince him he needs to leave.

The alien stopped and turned around. "If he volunteers to come with us, is that acceptable?"

Senator Johnston's smile vanished. "This isn't North Korea. This is America. If he wants to leave, that his right."

James snorted. "I'm not leaving. I'm sure they have shit barbeque in the Nine Systems Alliance."

Several soldiers laughed, and Shay cracked a smile.

"Then what is it?" the alien asked.

James gestured around at the soldiers, tanks, spaceship, and the alien. "First contact between the government and the Nine Systems Alliance. Fucking spaceship. A whole freaking army here. Short of me blowing up a building with perfect timing, this shit works. Spontaneous and all that. This shit is fucking epic."

Shay blinked. "No fucking way. You're kidding?"

James reached into his pocket and pulled out a ring box. He headed over to Shay and dropped to one knee. "Come on, Shay. It's not like you were gonna want fucking violins and doves." He opened the ring box to reveal a jade ring with ancient Chinese characters on it. "Shield ring. Works with the pendant I already gave you. Way stronger together."

Several soldiers cheered.

"Fuck, yeah. Go, Brownstone!" a man nearby yelled.

The alien frowned. "I don't understand. What's going on?"

Senator Johnston grinned. "You're seeing real Earth culture here right now."

Shay stared at the tattooed bounty hunter on one knee holding the ring in front of her. "You seriously want to propose to me surrounded by soldiers, an alien, tanks, and a senator?"

"Yeah." James grunted. "Before I met you, I didn't think about shit like love and marriage. Father McCartney said I should get married all the time because I obviously didn't have the personality to be a priest or monk. He shut up about it not all that long after you moved into my place. I guess he figured you'd be what I need." He smiled. "You know me, Shay. I'm good at ass-kicking and barbeque, not words. I know you thought I was gay when we first met, but you're damned beautiful. You kick ass. You're smarter than I am. And I love you. I don't think there's another woman on this planet, Oriceran, or any in the Nine Systems Alliance who is as perfect as you are for me. I know I don't always get what you want, and I'm never gonna claim I understand women, but I know my life means more now that you're in it, and I can't see you ever leaving it."

Shay stared at James, her breathing shallow. It was utterly and completely insane. Cracked. A marriage proposal at a semi-official first contact situation surrounded by heavily armed men was about the least romantic thing she could think of unless James added a few bodies to the mix.

But it was *fucking epic.*

Shay took the ring from James and slipped it over her finger. "Yes, Mr. Brownstone. I'll marry you."

More cheers erupted.

The alien watched the whole thing unfold with complete bafflement on his face and shook his head. "This planet is insane."

Senator Johnston cleared his throat. "I'd like an invite to that, by the way."

Shay winked at him. "I'm sure that can be arranged." She tugged on James' arms until he stood and leaned in to kiss him.

The senator turned back toward the alien. "Are we done here? I believe Mr. Brownstone and his fiancée were on their way to Las Vegas before you so rudely interrupted them."

The alien shook his head. "You humans are impossible. It might be the death of you." He turned and headed toward the ship.

"Don't you dare take that woman to a Vegas wedding chapel, James," the senator admonished. "Special women require special weddings."

James shrugged. "I figured she could handle the wedding planning. I nearly killed myself just trying to figure out a proposal."

Shay patted him on the arm. "Don't worry, I'll handle it all."

"Thank God."

The alien stepped inside his ship, and the walkway

retracted as the door closed.

Senator Johnston clapped his hands together. "Well then, that solves that. I'm sure in the next few weeks and months there'll be a lot of unusual diplomatic activity happening, but it won't be so bad, considering how things might have turned out."

"You would really have fought aliens to save me?" James looked surprised.

"If it wasn't for you being some Vax Forerunner thing, son, the Council would still be around. Every junkyard can use a mean dog." The senator smiled and pulled out his phone. "Now, if you'll excuse me, I have to make some calls. The alien dragnet we had out is costing a lot of money per day, and I think we made our point. You two have fun in Vegas." He narrowed his eyes on James. "And I meant what I said about the quickie marriage, son."

"Don't worry," Shay assured him. "There's no way I'd agree to that."

"Yeah," James rumbled. "Not like I can get Shay to do something she really doesn't want to do."

Senator Johnston stepped toward one of the soldiers in the back and gave them a wave. "Good lesson to learn right now, son. Happy wife, happy life."

The bottom thrusters of the Alliance ship kicked in and it rose, still eerily quiet.

James wrapped an arm around Shay, and they watched the ship as it ascended into the sky slowly for about ten seconds before shooting off in a blur.

"I like Spontaneous James," Shay murmured. "I like him a lot."

CHAPTER TWENTY-SIX

Senator Johnston was looking through some files on his computer when his door opened and a man in a dark suit entered. The man closed the door behind him and placed a small metallic cube on the edge of his desk. Even if he didn't recognize the man, he knew exactly where he was from.

"I've got privacy measures already," the senator explained, "Agent... You know what, I don't even want to know your name. It's easier that way. So many of you come and go."

The agent sat down across from him. "We're disappointed that you didn't coordinate the response with our teams. The President has some concerns as well with how things proceeded."

"Did I violate Protocol 2038 in any way, son?"

"No, but that's not the point." The other man frowned. "The point is, we suspected Brownstone was of non-Oriceran extraterrestrial origin, but now we know, and we also know that he's from a potentially very dangerous race. That's not something we can just ignore."

Senator Johnston snorted. "And I'll say to you what I told that Nine Systems man. He's *our* sonofabitch."

"How can you be so sure?"

"Because he has had plenty of time to go bad already. And I should think you and all the people in your little shadow ops groups would understand why we need an asset like him. Right now the opening communications with the Alliance are going okay, but today's ally can be tomorrow's enemy. They're afraid of Brownstone, and that's good because he's a loyal American who is also conveniently an alien supersoldier who has tangled with their operatives and won."

The agent eyed the senator with suspicion. "You want to use him as some sort of anti-alien backup?"

"I think having a large number of options is always good when you're worried about defense, especially against enemies who are stronger than you by default. The Oricerans are going to look out for themselves, first and foremost. Their magical advantage over us is huge, and from what I understand about how the way the gates work, it might take hundreds of years for that to equalize." Senator Johnston leaned back in his chair. "The cold truth is, we never had World War III because of nukes. Just think of James Brownstone as a nuke who thinks."

"Is that wise? He's already known to not trust the government, and he's a man who doesn't always play by the rules." The agent's frown deepened. "His fiancée is dangerous, too."

"If we continue to cultivate a good relationship with

him, he'll be there when it counts, just like he was with the Council." Senator Johnston pointed at his monitor. "And the Nine Systems Alliance admits they aren't the only group of aliens out there. Besides different organizations and alliances, there are also the Vax."

"That's what I really don't understand. We should be examining Brownstone and figuring out what makes him tick. Maybe developing biological weapon countermeasures—that sort of thing. If the Alliance can't handle the Vax, we might not have any chance. We should force him if necessary."

"Did you listen to a single damned word I've just said, son? You don't go and kick a nuke to find out how it works. He's from some advanced race centuries, if not thousands of years, ahead of us. Having some fool doctor with delusions of grandeur poke him isn't going to do anything but piss Brownstone off."

The senator wanted to slap the man for his stupidity.

"Maybe we could put leverage on his fiancée," the agent suggested. "Or his daughter."

Senator Johnston burst out laughing. "Are you *trying* to be stupid, son? The best way to piss off James Brownstone is to go after the people he cares about. He's already sore at the government for what went down during his daughter's adoption. You pressure her at all, we'll lose him forever." His smile disappeared. "If I find at any point that your people have screwed with Alison Brownstone or Shay Carson? Well, let's just not go there, shall we? You don't last long around Washington and these dark projects without knowing a thing or two about dealing with people who go against you. Do I make myself clear?"

The agent glared at the senator and gave him a curt nod. "So, your big plan is to be nice to Brownstone? That's what you're basing the security of the United States and Earth on?"

"Being nice and showing proper respect goes a long way. James is many things, but he's a man who understands when someone's done him a favor. The US government, through me, almost declared war on an alien civilization to defend him from being kidnapped. So, yes, I *do* think he'll be grateful."

"And if you're wrong?" The agent raised an eyebrow in question.

"Then we better have a mess of wizards ready to send him to the World in Between, and a whole army to push him there." Senator Johnston gave the agent a stern look.

"And what if the Vax come looking for him? What if they threaten his family or Earth?"

"Then God have mercy on their poor, sad souls because James Brownstone certainly won't."

AUTHOR NOTES - MICHAEL ANDERLE
JANUARY 3, 2019

THANK YOU for not only reading this story but these *Author Notes* as well.

(I think I've been good with always opening with "thank you." If not, I need to edit the other *Author Notes!*)

RANDOM (*sometimes*) THOUGHTS?

Proposals... So, today I had to admit to my wife that I was tearing up when reviewing the edited version of this story and the proposal scene. I felt the emotions that I hope some of you shared with me as Shay and Brownstone finally made official.

Two people, changed for the better because of love. My man Brownstone is all grown up, and the story has been told. Everyone (who is anyone) knows who and what James Brownstone is.

And he is going to get married!

However, DON'T you believe that we have delivered all the fun, because there is still something waiting in the wings (in about 3 books) to share.

It will be epic ;-)

HOW TO MARKET FOR BOOKS YOU LOVE

We are able to support our efforts with you reading our books, and we appreciate you doing this!

If you enjoyed this or ANY book by any author, especially Indie-published, we always appreciate if you make the time to review a book, since it lets other readers who might be on the fence to take a chance on it as well.

AROUND THE WORLD IN 80 DAYS

One of the interesting (at least to me) aspects of my life is the ability to work from anywhere and at any time. In the future, I hope to re-read my own *Author Notes* and remember my life as a diary entry.

Thursday late morning, Hilton Bali.

I am sitting across from Judith as I work and she is finishing breakfast. I'm in the Hilton Bali Resort and outside is...a bunch of fucking water.

I have JUST realized that I don't know which ocean is outside. This reminds me of the time I was staring at the Mediterranean thinking it was the Atlantic because I didn't know where Barcelona was in Spain.

Until two (2) minutes ago, I didn't know where I was in Bali, either.

It's the Indian Ocean, I believe.

Now, at least I have a name for the body of water.

I'm so location-ignorant sometimes. Who knew my lack of knowledge about world geography would be on display for hundreds (or thousands) to learn? Here's a tip, kids: use Google Maps. Don't Be Like Mike.

FAN PRICING

If you would like to find out what LMBPN is doing and the books we will be publishing, just sign up at http://lmbpn.com/email/. When you sign up, we notify you of books coming out for the week, any new posts of interest in the books and pop culture arenas, and the fan pricing on Saturday.

Ad Aeternitatem,

Michael Anderle

OTHER SERIES IN THE ORICERAN
UNIVERSE:

Other series in the Oriceran Universe:
THE DANIEL CODEX SERIES
I FEAR NO EVIL
THE UNBELIEVABLE MR. BROWNSTONE
SCHOOL OF NECESSARY MAGIC
THE LEIRA CHRONICLES
REWRITING JUSTICE
THE KACY CHRONICLES
MIDWEST MAGIC CHRONICLES
SOUL STONE MAGE
THE FAIRHAVEN CHRONICLES

OTHER BOOKS BY JUDITH BERENS

CONNECT WITH MICHAEL ANDERLE

Michael Anderle Social
  Website:
  http://www.lmbpn.com

Email List:
  http://lmbpn.com/email/

Facebook Here:
  https://www.facebook.com/OriceranUniverse/
  https://www.
facebook.com/TheKurtherianGambitBooks/